THE
MATTER
IS
LIFE

J. CALIFORNIA COOPER

THE
MATTER
IS
LIFE

C. 1

(DOUBLEDAY) 1991

NEW YORK   LONDON   TORONTO   SYDNEY   AUCKLAND

PUBLISHED BY DOUBLEDAY
a division of Bantam Doubleday Dell Publishing Group, Inc.
666 Fifth Avenue, New York, New York 10103

DOUBLEDAY and the portrayal of an anchor with a dolphin are
trademarks of Doubleday, a division of Bantam Doubleday Dell
Publishing Group, Inc.

Designed by Anne Ling

Library of Congress Cataloging-in-Publication Data

Cooper, J. California.
  The matter is life: stories / J. California Cooper.—1st ed.
    p.   cm.
  I. Title.
PS3553.O5874M37   1991
813'.54—dc20   90-25515
                                                                CIP

ISBN 0-385-41173-1
Copyright © 1991 by J. California Cooper
All Rights Reserved
Printed in the United States of America
July 1991
1   3   5   7   9   10   8   6   4   2
FIRST EDITION

ACKNOWLEDGMENTS

To all those of you who have encouraged and supported me.
I need that.

My daughter, Paris, who lifts me with her support and love.

My sister, Shy, who actually reads my work!

Warren D. Smith, who runs hither and yon, doing things for
me so I will have the peace and support to do my work.

To Robbie Lee of Black Heritage Art Gallery in Houston,
who saves and points out all those beautiful, emotion-filled
paintings to me. They provoke new thoughts and give me
more people to tell about and love.

To Temma Kaplan, Barnard College, for her large, generous
kind heart full of thoughtful doings. Barbara Tatum, Barnard College, for her sweet, thoughtful kindnesses.

Amistad Bookplace of Houston, Texas. Thank you Rosa and
Denice for all the valuable help you have given me.

To Reid Boates and Karen and the two little sons that make
Reid the most wonderful man/agent I know.

To the wonderful people of my last publisher—Michael Den-
neny, Michele Hinkson, Sarah, Keith, all of them who were,
and are, always so considerate and kind.

To the most wonderful new people of my new publisher, Doubleday—Sallye Leventhal, Evelyn Hubbard, Arabella, Heidi, Tina, Nancy and others, for their encouragement, faith and, yes, thoughtful kindnesses. I hope never to let them down. Martha Levin, too!

To Jehovah God. Oh, what would I do without Him?

AUTHOR'S NOTE

I give a lot of thought to the matter of Life. I mean to make mine as good and easy as possible. I stay as close to God and His wisdom as possible.

Some people say it takes courage to face the matter of death. Then . . . we are all courageous. Facing death, inevitably, to the end of our lives. Every day.

I believe it takes more courage to face Life. To survive the everyday matters of the mind, body and heart. Every minute is of great moment in the matter of Life. There may be no small matters. A penny piece of candy can choke you to death, like a penny piece of lover can kill your soul. A person alive at two o'clock may be dead at two ten, accidentally, from a wrong decision. A simple thing like boredom (which is really not simple) can create havoc in a life; it has the power to destroy. All in Life there is to decide upon is important to our living, in that it determines the quality, even the length, of our days.

Some people spend their lives in prisons.

Some, in the prison of Drugs . . . or Sex . . . Alcohol . . . Loveless Unions . . . in Hate . . . or Greed . . . even sell themselves, their lives.

There is Loneliness, Losing and Lack (and more).

There is Love, Laughter and Longevity (and more).

Everyone wants to matter.

Everyone wants to know what the matter is.

So . . . I name this book what I believe.

That, Always, no matter what the matter is . . .

THE MATTER IS LIFE

CONTENTS

THE BIG DAY

Every morning when I raise my head up from the bed, I say to myself, "Another morning. Good morning!" Then I slowly get up and commence my day. Cept this mornin . . . I lay awhile to talk to myself.

I am a frightfully old woman, somewhere near up to ninety years old. I don't know and I don't care no more. I'm older'n everybody else anyway!

But this day was a different kinda day cause it was the big day, a funeral day of a old, old man friend of mine who had lived to be ninety somethin years old too! Had a good life tho, cause he had a good wife, a young wife. Young for him. She bout fifty-five or fifty-six years old.

He had done married when he was forty-five or so, to a young, pretty girl bout sixteen years old. Everybody called him a fool cause of that and cause he was always laughin, smilin or teasing. Was a fine fellow to be around. A lot of fun. She, his wife, just wanted to get way from that house full of children at her home, and never enough money for nothin or nobody!

But he fooled em! He made that girl happy and kept her on up to now. Forty-five years. Somethin like that. They had some children, way grown now, and they stayed together. He been sick and down these last five, six years. But that woman . . . cause that's what she is . . . took such care of him, with such love that I seldom seen anywhere in my life and you already know I been here a long time.

Just think, if I'd a married him, I'd a had somebody to keep these old bones warm all these years my bed been empty. But . . . he wasn't the man for me . . . I wasn't the girl for him. I picked my own man, he died. Another one, I left that triflin fool and he was the best lover. Another one, we was together a long while, he wasn't no real good lover, but he was a good man. He died. I was tired then. Nuff, enough.

Anyway, today my old friend's funeral, his big day. We all got to go, cause when you gets his age you know everybody and they know you. Sides that, his laughter made him lovable.

Anyway. What was I sayin? I ain't ready for all this talkin. Cause I'm sad. I hate to see people I like die, but I like funerals cause then I get to see people I ain't seen in a long time. And all the new ones too. My memory was always good, ain't changed a bit so I see from where all them people

been to where they done come to. I like that, when it don't
make me sad. You be surprised how many things I knew was
gonna turn out like they did! Sure nuff!

Anyway, this morning my grandchile, or great
grandchile, was in the kitchen stiring things up for fixin. She
hollered to me, cause I'm the slowest one, "Biggun!"

They use to call me "Mama," then "Big Mama, then
there was so many mamas in between, they just call me
"Biggun" now. I don't 'low no "granmaw" stuff cause it
sounds like somethin you snatch off a hog.

I called back to her, "I ain't ready."

She looked round my door. "Time now, Biggun. I be in
to wash you up in a few minutes and get you some breakfast."

I gave her a mean look cause they spect that. Said, "Told
you I ain't ready."

She laughed, said, "You never ready to do nothin somebody want you to do. Now, get to gettin up."

I smiled to myself, cause I am loved, chile.

The early morning went by, everybody gettin ready to
go. Me, I'm the longest, slowest one. I sit, or open drawers
and stare in em for awhile, then shut the drawer. Done forgot what I was after. Maybe I open another one, cause I like
to see what's in em. Or I go to my closet and pull that
curtain back and stare in there. I ain't lookin for nothin to
wear. They gon see to that. I be just lookin at all the fine,
new things that love done brought me. Them children always
buyin me somethin nice. Specially the ones is away. These
here, too, but these here DO things for me. Things I really
need. I done forgot, with all this good memory of mine,

which of my grandchildren blong to which child of mine. But I do know each man each child of mine blongs too!

Well. Now, they all ready. I ain't. They done washed me, dressed me, sat me, combed me, brushed me, all like that. I rather do it myself, but they rather do it too. After I fuss awhile, tellin em I ain't ready, and I ain't, I let em do things cause I like to feel their hands on me. Hand touch of love.

I hear em gettin the little ones in the car. I sit down. They hollar for me. I hollar back, "I ain't ready." And I mean it this time! Cause I don't want to go to his funeral after all. Cause I know mine bout be next. They come in and get me and I get on out, fussin. But everybody look so pretty and bright, I smile, then laugh at em and with em.

Well, now, we drive down these roads I use to walk barefoot on and love to see, even now. I see all these big, tall trees and all them thickets and wild flowers in all them pretty, wild colors. Back of all that is the wild blue sky, fulla them big fat clouds justa floatin up there all free and fulla water, not worrin bout dyin at all. And everytime I go out, I notice some new little houses wasn't there last time I went that way. So you can see these people don't never take me nowhere too much.

By and by, we gets to the Big Church. It's a little church with big leanings. Wood old, wire old, pipes old, piano old, but good. Preacher old, choir mixed up . . . good. I like a good choir and I sure like a good piano. Seems like I got one playin in my heart when I hear em.

They always sits me where I can be sure and see everybody and everybody can see me and tell me how good I look. I always answer em, "I ain't ready to look no other way!"

It gets real crowded. He was a good man. Course, lots of

em here are all related. Well, we all is in some way, cause it's a lot of sneakin done down here cause it's a small town. Just like all over the world, I reckon.

I look at the crowd. See all those beautiful colors, faces and clothes. Ahhhhhhh. These womens is wearin Sunday best. The widow has got on a bright yellow dress with large white flowers in it, but her face looks like a flower that died. Poor chile. I look back at the crowd and see more bright yellows, glowing reds, deep blues, smooth greens, even some of that aqua color, some black, few purple, lotta white dresses on little children. And all them mixed colors justa moving and sparklin in the sun. My dress is a pretty gray. The mens is mostly in blues and blacks and gray suits. I pay them no mind. I like to thrill my eyes with the other colors that seem alive as they burst in and wake up my dim eyes.

I look at all the fine, bright clothes on some of the young and old strong bodies. Some don't look just right cause the woman's arms are muscled and strong from pullin and hoein cotton, pullin corn, washin by hand and wringin them big heavy sheets and quilts out. Reachin for distant berries, pullin greens, and workin in the cabbage patch. Strong arms, strong backs, muscles in legs strong from pushin and pullin not only things, but life. Sweat already under some arms, I see. Some of these clothes was meant to be for little frail weak, stylish lady-like bodies. I see a ruffle on a strong corded neck, a crocheted collar coverin the shoulders of a woman who plows for herself. She probly crocheted that collar, too.

Anyway they's all greetin each other and holdin hands, shakin heads, rollin eyes, laughin. Plenty kisses and huggin them that done come from a long way off, least bout 150 miles or so! Some more, some less.

It's some white folks here, too. One old white couple I know was his true friends and the other three white men was them I recognized as them who done stole much of the oil and lumber land from some of these same people sittin right here in the church next to em! Come to make friends with the widow, I reckon. See what she got they can get!

Wellll, they done filled the church now and all a sudden they done got serious and sad. Cause the widow is so sad and cryin, standin by the casket of her forty-five-, fifty-year husband. I blive I'm countin right. After enough years, who counts anyway?

She still a young woman, just done got a little ugly with time and hard work and children, just livin. She still young. Bout fifty somethin, I guess. I wish I was fifty one more time! But now . . . she alone. Like me. Enh! Ehn!

Everybody seated and pattin dresses and children down and straight.

The piano started! ♫ Good player! It's a good song. I done forgot what it was. The choir sings. At first you don't want them to join in and mess up that good piano, but after they start, you glad they did, cause they good, too! ♪ ♪ ♪ ♪ ♪

Then the solo woman came on. A medium size woman, brown, hair smoothed close to her head in them little oily curls full with sweat now, a wide gap tween her teeth that had a little gold on em. Had a good, strong deep voice full of sorghum syrup, blackberry juice, collard greens and plenty of pain. That woman sent me somewhere! That she was holdin on to God and her man was all in the cracks of her voice. I heard it! I know the sound! Of a woman who loves her God, and her man and who thinks she is ugly, big and awkward cept with one thing, a beautiful voice. She use it every time she can, so her man can hear it . . . and forget that other pretty woman who won't let him lone. And that other woman ain't really so pretty either, just pretty to his wife cause she wants her husband! ♬ ♪

When they done moaned and laid everybody back with the like of that, the preacher step slowwwly up to the pulpit. Got a microphone in the Big Church now. He talk about the scriptures. People commence to sayin, "Sure nuff. Lord!" and things like that. Some hollar, "Mercy!" Well, everybody know what they need. ♩

Then he talk about the dead man in the coffin, while I hears the piano playin ♪ softly in the background. ♪ But I hear, too, the pattin of the feet some people is playin out their feelin's with. ♩

♪ Slow ones. . . . Pat . . . . pat . . . . . pat . . . . . pat . . . . . pat . . . . . pat . . . . . pat. The ones with full hearts. . . . Pat . . . pat . . . pat . . . pat . . . pat . . . pat . . . pat. Hurt ♪ ones. . . . PATPATPATPATPATPATPATPAT. ♪ ♩ And a moan, now and then, to let go some pain. Piano still playin ♩ softly.

Preacher take the text somewhere in John 14. Say . . . "Jesus goin somewhere to prepare a place for YOU." And after he talk about the many mansions, he step slowwwwwly back and sit down.

"Yes Lord." "My God." "Hummmm-hummmm." Through sorrow or memory.

Then the white minister, cause the dead man had some white relations round here, he got up and took the pulpit and said a prayer for the family. Was a nice one. Said, "May God keep them."

I said to myself, "He betta, cause we needs help, higher help, in this here world." Then he sat back down.

Then I snapped to! Cause the piano rose up ♫, ♪ higher, tho still softly, ♪ and the music just softly boomed out. ♪ Them high ups ♩ and low down notes ♫ just stole out and ♪ jumped out from round under them hands playin ♪ that piano, stole into your heart, ♩ then down to some feet. Men's big feet go a deeper sound from a woman's smaller foot. I listens. ♫ Patpatpatpatpatpat. PAT . . . PAT . . . PAT. ♪ Some folks did their pattin with both feet, one at a time. Pat . . . Pat. Pat . . . Pat. Pat . . . Pat. Pat . . . pat.

Now the last preacher got up and walked to the pulpit lookin into everybodies eyes. He had a deep-crackin reachdown voice, sad today. I can't member all he said, but I know I remembered what I like best.

"No need to say good-by. We will all meet again." I member too, he said, "Ain't no need to be playin round with your time here, thinkin it won't happen to you. . . . Cause it will. And only YOU know where you goin. Be careful what you pack in your suitcase of life, cause that's what you gonna take with you. Watch that double dealin malice, that hate and greed. Adultry and lyin. Sex and gossip that you put in it, cause it gets heavy and you can't get far with it."

Oh! The feets went to pattin so fast was like a little tiny army was passin through the church. I was worried bout the floor, but when he was through, the church was still standin. Done weathered many a these storms, I guess.

Then the piano went into my favorite! "Precious Lord,

♪ take my hand, Lead me on, help me stand." ♪ Oh! She hit on them bass keys ♪ and rolllllllled. ♪ She rolled through the storm. ♪ The storm rolled to the end. ♪ Them pattin feet rolled. ♪ The hands clap, couldn't hold still. ♪ The eyes rolled up to heaven. The tears rolled down to the earth. ♪ Movin to the music. ♪

She kept playin softly now. ○ The people moaned softly now, as the preacher read the Twenty-third Psalm. Then he said, with his fingers tappin on the pulpit thing, "Life is like your shadow . . . you can't get away from what you do. You look back . . . it's gonna be there. You betta keep your hand in the hand of God. YOU know when you doin your best."

Then the piano rolled ♪ out again ♪ and the people went in lines to pass by and view their friend, their relative, the man in the coffin, for the last, last time. They went to raise me up, I said, "I ain't ready!" They let me lone.

Then it was over and everybody was goin out the door. They finally got me out, after three or four "ain't ready's." Oh such a huggin and a kissin goin on out there in the sun. People askin round, "What your family name? Ain't I kin to you?" More hugs and kisses.

Mostly all told me how good I looked and got around for my age. Some I smiled at, some I told, "Poot on that! If you ain't goin nowhere, just goin from the bed to the toilet to the porch, back to the bed, restin all the time, you sposed to look good!" We all laugh.

Then it's time to get in the cars and go to eat at the widow's house and really get down to talkin and gossip, old and new. They didn't have to make me now, I was ready. Cause I love to eat! You see?

When that was all over, I was full of everybody's chicken and roast and ham, corn and peas. I got a child to get me a paper plate and I kept tellin them good-cookin women to reach me a piece of they cake or pie to take home. They did, and I had a good load of sweets. Gonna take my teeth out and suck on this stuff all through the day and night.

They come to get me, told me we was goin and tried to take my plate, covered now, but I held on to it, still lookin round the table. Told em "I ain't ready." But they got me anyway.

We all went home full, and a little quiet. Just somebody sayin, "That was Gurline Burn, you remember her?" Or bout somebody comin up from someplace. Things like that. We rode home a little sad, a little happy, a little full of spirit, a little tired.

I knew, and pictured in my mind some of them, who came from out of this town, was somewhere right then packin pecans, greens, corn, preserves, things like that, in bags and boxes, takin some of their home home with them.

We passed Big Church on the way home and I stared at it, even turned round in my seat, lookin at it out the window as long as I could see it. Wonderin, sayin to myself, "Won't be long now. My time probly next, cause nobody don't last forever. Seein my last stop on my way to the grave." I turned back round, stole a little piece of potato pie out the side of my plate.

Home, they told me to go change clothes cause it been a long day for me.

I told em, "I ain't ready! Cause it ain't been no long day for me! Ain't no day too long for me no more."

After I was in bed, I lay there thinkin bout the widow,

God, Life, while I was eatin from my plate I had done hid in my drawer next to the bed. My teeth sittin in a cup on top the stand watchin me gum that food to pieces.

I always say, "Well, we got another night. Good night," to myself. Then I say a prayer to God fore I go to sleep.

This time, I told God, "You can call on me do You get ready to. But, I'm gonna tell You right now, just like I been tellin You for years now. Just so You don't forget, so You know in time. I AIN'T READY!"

I hear my daughter, one, callin, tellin me to go to sleep and quit all that talkin in here to myself. I put another piece of sweet in my mouth, said "I ain't ready!" just fore I fell off to sleep. Makes me so mad when I do that, cause I wasn't ready!

HOW, WHY TO GET RICH

LESSON #1

You know, I'm just a kid, but I got nerves, and sometimes grown-up people just really get on em! Like always talkin about how kids don't have no sense "in these days." Like they got all the last sense there was to get. Everybody with some sense knows that if grown-up people had so much sense the whole world wouldn't be in the shape it's in today!

Cause don't nobody in the world seem to get along together, nowhere. Not even here, where they sposed to have most of the sense!

I came up, long with some war. It's so many wars you can't always remember which one. My mama and daddy moved to the big city to get rich workin at one of them shipyards. Gramma too. It was real exciting coming, drivin all cross the country of the United States. Coming to where the streets was paved with gold and all everybody was makin money. We was gonna save up a lot of it and go home. Change our lives, Daddy said. Get rich.

Well, we didn't get rich or nothing like it. We got changed, tho. We got a lot of other things, too. Like separated and divorced. Daddy met one of them ladies out from under one of them weldin hats was workin at the shipyard. And Mama was sweet-talked, or somethin, by somebody else was workin in the same shipyard! They sposed to be makin boats and ships and things down there and it look like they mostly made love and troubles, breakin up families!

Daddy's lady liked to party and stuff, so lotta our saving money went out that way. And him and Mama began to fuss and fight a lot, with Gramma runnin round sayin, "Now you all, now you all. . . ." But it didn't help nothin.

Then, Mama put him out and locked the door one night after he got off the "night shift." See, he really worked days. We had to move then, cause our money was cut in half or just even way down.

After while we moved into some cockroach's house. I don't know was it because of bein poor or nothin, maybe just cause it so crowded round here. Ain't hardly no place to rent near bout nice as our house what we was buyin back home what we left from to come out here and get rich.

Mama kept workin, naturally, and Gramma took to workin part-time domestic. It was just the three of us then, but things were high-priced and soon Gramma had to work full-time cause Daddy didn't bring no money much.

You could see everybody if you stayed out in the streets long enough, so I used to hang around places where he might be going to. Bars, gamblin shacks, Bar-B-Q shops. When I see him on the street he would always go in his pocket and give me some money, a big kiss and a hug. But not Mama. He wouldn't give her nothin, he said, cause she had a man-friend now. I didn't see no sense in that cause I was his child and he was the only man-friend in my life. Help me! But he didn't, if I didn't catch him.

Gramma didn't like Mama's man-friend so, soon, Mama was stayin away over to his room and it was just Gramma and me. Gramma tryin to work and make me a home so I'd be a good girl and grow up to be a good woman, and me tryin to catch my daddy on the streets with his bad woman for that extra five or ten dollars he would give me. This new place didn't have no streets paved with gold for us, but it sure did change our life. If I was a cussin person I could tell you what my Gramma says the streets are paved with!

Then, Gramma's other children who had come out here started havin problems too. Either the mama or the daddy left and each one sent their children to live with us. With us! There was two, both boys.

Our life changed some more. Scuffelin round with Gramma on what chores everybody else ought to do, who ate the most, got the dirtiest jobs and things like that. We all went to school. And we were poorer than ever. People sure can forget their kids! Just love em and leave em. They knew we had to eat and Gramma was workin hard as she could. We was poor. Government said we wasn't, but it sure felt like poor to us!

About this gettin rich, it's very easy to understand why

19

anyone wants to be rich. One big reason, for us, was we was poor, black and living in a ghetto. All three of us, my two fourteen-year-old boy cousins and thirteen-year-old me, were single children. That is we had one parent each . . . Gramma.

I will call one "John" (the slick one) and the other one "Doe" (the kinda dumb one), and you can call me "Einstein" cause I was the smart one. Now Doe had come from the country, but John and me were from the city; leastways, a little city close to a big City. We always had the ideas, Doe was a hard worker, but very lazy at it.

Anyway, going on a paper route in the mornings (I went along to manage things because my grandmother had to have absolute peace and quiet to sleep as late as she could before we helped her cook breakfast and she went to work), we always saw this gang of people on the street corner. Befuddled, dirty, poor-lookin, some winos, stuff like that, waiting for the bus to haul them to the country to pick fruit or something like that all day. Then they would be brought back to the same corner where they all began to stuff their hands in their pockets, hunch their shoulders and walk hurriedly away, kinda a tired hurry.

Now, we knew they must have made some money and were rushing off to buy things with it! So, one morning I asked the bus driver how the job went, you know, how much and all? Well, he said fifteen cents a sack or a box depending on what was picked. That sounded pretty good to me when I thought of my two big strong cousins, so I asked what we had to do to get the job. The answer was to get a social security card and be on the corner at 5:00 A.M.

I thought about that for a week or so, then held a meeting and we all went down and lied and got our social security cards. I said I was twenty-six years old, so you know that was some government worker who wasn't thinking bout nothin cause she gave me my card and after my two cousins lied, gave em theirs, too!

We rushed home and explained everything to our grandmother, who listened and laughed a little when she told us that was hard work. Wellll, we know ALL work was hard to her so that didn't stop us!

She gave us some money to buy bologny and some other stuff after we arranged to pay her back. We fixed our lunches in the best happy mood we had been in, in a long time! We made a beautiful fat bologny sandwitch each and a piece of fruit; set them neatly in the refrigerator with our names printed neatly on each bag. We then went to bed to sleep, dreamin of all the money we were going to have!

I even counted up to maybe a year between the three of us and we could let me keep the money, some of it, save it and then maybe find a little business we could go into to get away from cockroach alley, the dirty looking characters and the winos round here. Set Gramma down. Not have to wait around waitin to catch my daddy. I had all our lives planned. I slept good that night!

Anyway, we woke up early, ate a little cold cereal, grabbed our lunches and rushed to the corner. Wellll, the bus was halfway down the block, leaving us! We screamed and hollored, but to no avail, cause he kept right on truckin. Oh! We were mad! And disgusted! After we got through blaming each other, we went home and got ready to eat our lunches when Gramma told us we better save em for the next day if we was gonna try again cause she wasn't buying no more! See? I knew I had to get rich! We sat the lunches in the refrigerator and went on out to get the papers we had stashed and deliver them to the people who almost didn't get them!

The next morning we skipped the cereal and rushed to the corner, but they were gone again! My Lord!! We were mad! We went home and put our lunches back in the frig. You know them sandwitches were beginning to turn up at the edges! Much less the fruit! We ate that soggy fruit stuff on the way home in the dark morning. We hardly spoke for half a day or so . . . we all blamed each other.

The next morning, the THIRD one, we didn't even go to the bathroom or nothin. Went to bed dressed and ready and got up, grabbed them beat-out tired lunch bags and made it to the bus . . . on time.

Now, there was a very disgusting group we were goin with and we felt so superior to them mentally and physically. We knew we would be the champs that whole year and we laughed at them and everything! Especially one old lady who looked like she was 109 years old.

We just laughed at everything! We almost rolled in the aisle of the bus, but we kept it down except for that piece of laugh that sometimes busts out in spite of all you can do to hold it in!

One old wino-lookin man was telling everybody bout his experience as a picker and everything he said he would add, "Don't you know? Don't you know?" That cracked us up! We didn't listen to what he said, just how he said it. We found out later we shoulda just listened to what he was sayin.

Well, daylight was coming fast now, and the farther we

drove, the hotter it was gettin to be. It didn't look hot, but when that big, ole red sun shone down on you through that ole dusty window, it was hot! The scenery was nice tho. You know, space and trees and a big sky and all. To a city kid, it was different. It was good. Like back home. I had forgot I missed it, with all the other stuff I had to have on my mind. We finally just relaxed and enjoyed it. I know it's some birds in the city, but we could SEE these, justa flying way out all over in the sky. The tall trees wavin and stretchin, like us, in the morning sun. And the sky . . . the sky was so clear . . . and blue. I got so relaxed and dreamy, I even dozed off a few times. Doe slept. John was still sniggling at the old wino til I told him to quit it cause he was nudging me with his elbow, lettin me know to listen to somethin and all I wanted, at that time, was to look out the dirty window and dream about stuff.

Anyway after bout two hours or so, the bus arrived at a field and we stretched quickly and flexed our muscles and jumped off. We were ready! Ready to get started on our big money! Everybody else just walked off, natural like. We grabbed two or three sacks each and told the man to point to our part. He said, "You all kin take any part but just stay in this section." Okey!!

It was an onion field. We started right in diggin and pullin them onions to load our sacks just like we was throwin money in them sacks. We threw the extra sacks around our necks, but in two minutes that sun was so hot on our backs we threw them sacks off, watching where, so we would know how far we had to come back for them. We were organized!

Well, fifteen minutes later the bus driver came out and, waving his hands over his head, he hollered, "Wrong field, wrong field!" and pointed toward the bus to let us know to head back. Oh shit! we said to the sun (and we didn't even curse much usually). He continued, "Throw em down, leave em here!" We said to each other, "Not us! Hell, this is hard work!" Everybody else must have said the same thing cause everybody took a few onions out and threw them on the ground, then took their sacks on the bus with them. My cousin John, the city boy, grabbed all ours back when nobody was looking and some of the other ones too! He got on the bus with onions falling every-whichaway, saying they were all his.

Now, that onion smell . . . in that hot bus . . . was overpowering, so we were really glad to get to the right field. That took about ten minutes or so, then we were hopping out to get going again!

The sun wasn't even up very high, maybe it was about 9:30, but it was like it had been up there shining all week! I wanted to take some of my clothes off! But I'm a girl, and a lady, as my grandmama taught me, so I kept em on, even that thick cotton undershirt she had made me put on. Chile, I was hot!

We got started. The field was still onions. I stayed close to my cousins because the 109-year-old lady and I were the only two women and she didn't get no eye action, but the men seemed to look at me a lot from under their hats. See, I kinda had a little bust line, you know. So I was careful to stay close to protection should anybody lose their mind out there lookin at my new shape I was gettin! Anyway, now we could go to work for real.

Don't you ever let anyone tell you that an onion is smooth! You had to pull so hard to get them things out of the ground! My smooth, young skin started comin off on them onions. I went over to the bus man and asked for a knife to dig them with and he asked me, "How old are you?"

I lied, "Sixteen."

He said, "That ain't old enough, you have to be eighteen." He smiled with some yellow teeth between his cracked lips.

Darn! I hadn't lied enough! So I gave him a mean look and went on back to my row and my sack. I had about half a sack only. John and Doe were not too much further ahead of me, but everybody else was on their second row and their third or fourth bag! The 109-year-old lady even was workin on her third sack! Maybe she was only a hundred years old!

Well, anyway, at lunch time, two and a half hours later, I had a bag and a half. John had two bags and Doe had about two and a half! I know John had stole some of them onions from the other sacks when he went to start a new row. At fifteen cents a sack, we had made ninety cents! Altogether.

Ach! (This picking was teaching me how to speak German.) We only had three hours more to go and it was goin to cost us $1.25 each to pay for the bus trip! Ach! We hadn't asked Gramma for no money because that didn't make sense! WE were going to make plenty money! Besides, she would have screamed anyway. One, for waking her up, and two, for the money. The hundred-year-old lady had fifteen sacks. Fifteen! All by herself!

Lunch time. We got our lunch bags from the bus and looked for some shade. Quick as we wipe the sweat away it would come right back. It was hot, hot, HOT! I have to say it three times! We were hot, sweaty and dirty and tired. Oh Lord, we was tired. My hands were raw. The sack was heavy and only half-filled. I had to lug mine with me everywhere just to keep my own cousins from takin any. We looked at each other and we almost cried! But . . . we were too strong for that. Besides, nobody wanted to be first to cry. We all knew one thing tho . . . we HAD to get enough onions to get home. That $1.25 each!

We opened our lunch bags (under no shade) and those bologny sandwitches were almost rolls, they had turned up so far! The lettuce, an ugly shade of greenish-brown, we threw away. The tomato, we just sqwished and threw in the dirt (even the birds flew away from em). We ate at the rest.

Then a bean lunch truck drove up. Those beans were smelling GOOD! All over that field! And we didn't have any money! Now . . . I knew enough to know that some of those men had been eyeing me all day and so I just walked over to the bean truck and stood there lookin like a hungry fool. My cousins just stood back and watched me. Somebody beckoned me to the bean window, but I shook my head with the saddest face I could make, I wasn't playin either, and said I didn't have any money. After a little while, the wino-lookin older man bought me a bowl of beans. A whole bowl of beans! Oh! they smelled so good! I smiled down at them and almost screamed with delight as I walked away from the man, thanking him. I even forgot how hot and tired I was. Only for a minute tho.

I had swallowed two mouthfulls when I felt the heat from the peppers. The stuff was loaded with peppers! Flames seemed to, and did, come out on my breath! I wished I was still starvin again. I gave the bowl to my cousins who began to fight over it as I rushed to the water can! I was still drinking water when they got there in a little while and pushed me away from the water. Them beans was hot! Now we were burning up on the outside from the sun and on the inside from the beans. We were broke and had about six sacks between us! I went to sit on the bus, mad, to try to think this out, since I am the one with the brains. I snatched that paper contract we had signed, that the busman gave me a copy of, from my pocket and started to read the fine print. Could they leave us out there, God only knows where? If we didn't have the dollar twenty-five each? You had to pay them when they paid you, just before you left for home. Home. Oh, home, home, home. Oh, Gramma, Gramma, sweet Mama, sweet Daddy. I woulda cried cept I had to save my strength. But my heart felt like it was too big for my chest, and it hurt to swallow.

My associates came on the bus to get the lowdown and I gave it to them! We had to have the money. As we sat there, I looked out the window and saw the old lady; she had bout eighteen sacks or more now. That beat-up old lady! She had gone back to work early! She was taking care of her business. You know? I looked at that old lady and I respected her! I respected her because she was doing what she had to do and she was doing it good!

I turned back to my problems cause I meant to solve em and respect myself too.

I looked at my cousins . . . two of my problems! I told em where we all stood. Doe, the country cousin, went back out there and really started packing those onions. John, the city cousin, went out there to see whose onions he could steal; his eyes darting back and forth over the people in the field. My grandmama say you can just about tell who is gonna go to jail in life, just by watchin what people do in their daily livin. I began to understand her more. Then, I went to talk to the busman and show him my sore, raw hands, so I could get some sympathy and maybe a free ride home, but he was busy, he said, so I got my sack and started digging onions again, with tears in my eyes and evil in my heart!

I don't know where they got that song from, "Shine On, Harvest MOON," cause I will never forget that sun shining on me in that harvest. We really worked, tho. Doe was tryin to tear up those rows, and John was stealin so fast that a man stopped him and musta told him a few hard things that made him see the benefit of diggin his own onions cause he did work a few rows of his own for awhile. For awhile. No-body wanted to walk home after this hot, bone-tired day. We didn't talk, laugh or even smile anymore. Cause wasn't nothin funny no more.

Well . . . we got on the bus when it was time to go home. Somehow we had made it! We had thirteen cents over the fare. Don't ask me how. Just thirteen cents, thats all. We sat with our mouths poked out all the way home. Thinking hard.

We had never really thought about labor and unions and all that stuff. Or given too much attention to the civil rights movements, cause it didn't seem to touch us too much where we lived. But, now, we noticed there were not but two white people on the bus. All the rest of us were black, with a few mexicans, I guess, all colored in some way. But all poor, even the white ones.

I looked at that hundred-year-old lady who had worked so hard. She might have been twenty years old for all I knew. Just tired and wore out, thats all! A hundred years worth of tired! My respect grew and something else I didn't know what to call it.

I tried to give the man who had bought the beans for me the thirteen cents, but he just shook his head, "No." Said, "Help somebody else on down the road someday." Then cracked his face into a kinda smile and waved me on away.

We were even too tired to doze off after we were crumbled in our seats. We didn't see the trees and the sky on our way home. But I'm glad the space was out there . . . we needed it in that old, creaking, rattling, heaving bus that was hot and funky with the sweat of a hard day's "honest" work.

But there was something more . . . the smell of poor . . . the smell of somebody's home being worse than those fields. Some had packed a few onions in their pockets or lunch bags. What, I wondered, would they buy with that body-breaking little money to go with those onions? I felt something . . . something . . . but I don't know what it was. It was just there in my mind.

My grandmama, even my mama, my daddy had done this kinda work a little. I didn't want to talk about it. I just wanted to be quiet and feel it til I knew what it was. It felt a little like resignation . . . I seemed to catch it from the people in the bus. Something in me refused it. I changed it to indignation. For myself.

When we got off the bus at home, I knew why the people walked hurriedly away. To rest . . . and forget, until to-morrow or . . . death, I guess. I don't know. I only know that day has made me think so hard. So hard.

We started home with the thirteen cents. Somehow, I started crying and they almost did, until we started laughing. Then we each took a penny and threw it in the street. Then we almost cried again from our aching bones, til we laughed again. We finally got home and told Gramma about it. She laughed so hard at us, we got mad at her and cried til we couldn't help laughing at each other.

She made us bathe. We didn't want to, we just wanted to fall out in the bed. After, we were glad we had washed all the onion, dirt and sweat off. Gramma gave us a good hot meal, store bought, then we hit that bed and I believe I was sleep midair on my way to the pillow. Gramma said we all snored like old men.

We always have to go to church every Sunday, whether we feel like it or not because Gramma says we have to learn what road to take in life. Nowwww, I understand what that means, a little better, cause I'm not takin that road out to them fields again! Not if I can help it! We like God too, I guess, because when we really couldn't think of what to spend that dime on and how hard we had worked for it, we decided to give it to Him. I don't know what the preacher did with it, but we gave it to God.

I don't know what John and Doe thought, but I said a prayer for that hundred-year-old lady, then for the man who bought the beans, then broke down and included them all. But the last thing I said to God was, "Please, please, don't let me make my life like that. Please."

Lately, I pay more attention to the labor and black movements. Or just poor people movements. Maybe I would be a labor official or something where you have some say bout what you do. I don't know. All I do know is I don't ever want to go pick nothing in no field no more unless it is my field, my own. Or I was the boss.

You know, you don't have to be white to be president of

anything. Even of the United States. I could be president! Black as I am! And if you white and poor, you don't have to be rich to get to be president either.

I could be president! Even being a girl, a lady. Cause some of these laws and rules got to be changed!

I think about life too . . . my mama . . . my daddy. Maybe there is a reason or something for why they act like they do when they be working and tryin to make a livin. Separating and divorcin and all. They got to go out there and do it everyday! Work! I only did it for one day . . . and I was so tired and evil. I even cried, only for a minute tho.

Oh, I don't know. But I understand more what my grandmama is tryin to teach me. I remember that hundred-year-old lady!

Yea. I think about all those things now.

I think I'm gonna hate onions for a long, long time, too. And dumb boys.

Yes . . . I'm doing a lot of thinking. On how to get rich. Even just how to make a real good livin for my life! Cause I already know why.

EVERGREEN
GRASS

I am a old, old lady and I know a lot of old, old sayins that I know to be true cause I done lived long enough to see em out to be so. Some sayins ain't nothin but smart-soundin words that make out like they know what they talkin bout, but some of em is really sure enough true.

Like, the grass is always greener on the other side of the fence. You got to watch that grass! Or maybe you oughta just watch your own grass and keep that green! Cause that grass on the other side will fool you sometime. Look greener while it be dyin all the time.

See, I don't live far from one or two families out here in the country and I have in mind one couple I knew for a long time. Can't even spell their name right, but when you say it, it sound like Gunioff.

Mr. Gunioff had made his way up from the bottom by havin built a solid farm, married, had children, raised them and finally waved good-by to them as they went out into the world to seek their own fortunes. He then settled back with Mrs. Gunioff to enjoy a good solid middle age to death. They was both quiet people, tho he more than she. She did like to go to church and little community social events and things like that which didn't interest him none at all! She was a slight-built woman, gray-haired, neat, sweet. She was friendly with the neighbors, the closest ones bein the couple up the road apiece, the Conets.

Mrs. Conet was a little youngish, brown-skinned, very nice lookin woman. Mr. Conet was hardworkin, quiet, dark-brown man. Always courteous. Went to church a lot with his wife, like he used to go with his mama. Reason I mention them, is cause I happen to know that Mrs. Conet was a fussy little woman, always comparin her husband and everything he did to all the other men round here. Nothin was enough for her. But I guess he loved her cause he put up with all her fussin and complainin. Half the time she didn't know what she was talkin bout. Like to run that man crazy, I magin. The other half the time, I don't know bout cause I live closer to the Gunioff family, so I saw them more.

He, Mr. Gunioff, liked to fool with his sheep and cows and his horse and the chickens and his dog. Gently taciturn, he was bored with much of life and he was, of course, boring.

What first comes to my mind is the day he drove his wagon one bright morning, returning from town where he had purchased some poison to set out for the animal that had killed one of his sheep. As he drove he noticed the green fields he loved and the blue of the sky with the birds flyin overhead. He enjoyed the sight of the birds ever so much more then the shootin of them for sport. He could smell the air . . . all was good. All, that is, except for the animal who had killed his sheep. Oh, well, he was going to fix that!

When he arrived home he waved the package containing the leg of lamb at Mrs. Gunioff, who nodded back from her sewing, and went to the kitchen to prepare the poison. He carved into the lean red meat and as it separated so smoothly, he felt a sense of pleasure and made several extra slices and holes in the meat before he realized he had enough and began to stuff the poison into the open parts thinkin all the time of how he would stop this menace before it went too far. Some damn wolf or something eatin his stock! He sat everything out later that evenin and went to bed early with his gun and a lantern by the door so if he heard any noise he could get up and out and see what was goin on with no time wasted.

Bedtime was early for both Gunioffs and he had slept lightly for bout an hour or so, when he was awakened by sounds from the yard. He rushed up and out, grabbing his lantern and gun as he did, running softly as possible to the place he had set the trap.

The wild animal there had eatin most of the leg of lamb right there without takin it away and was now in the throes of death. Its body jerked and writhed over the ground. Its eyes bulged and glared, its mouth was foamin while painful gutteral sounds came out. Mr. Gunioff watched fascinated.

He set the lamp down without thinkin and knelt down to stare at the dyin animal. He watched to the end.

When it was over he probed the beast with his foot to try to get him to move again, but its body had twisted itself into the stillness of death. Mr. Gunioff stared at it for a long time then hearing Mrs. Gunioff calling from the house to see if he was alright, he waved back and then drug the beast away to bury him.

He thought about the death he had seen all that week and looked often at the bag of poison he had left.

One day, feeding the sheep, he noticed the sickly one and the thought squoze into his mind that it need not live. He should poison it! Put it out of its misery! He could see one more time the workings of this poison that made the victim dance such a strange dance. That night he prepared the poison but waited til daybreak so he could see the dance better. He fed the sickly sheep off by itself and stood entranced, fascinated, watching it go through the labor of death.

He began to sit on the porch through the day, even more quiet than usual. He didn't even go to one of the few things he ordinarily would go to with his wife. One day she dressed in her little country clothes and went off in the wagon with the Conet couple that lived down the road. That was the day he went out and searched among the sheep and found one he thought would not last long anyway and fed it the poison and watched it die!

Later that week as he sat on the porch he decided sheep were too expensive to lose and turned his face to the chicken yard, wondering how they would dance. He soon found reason to go to town and did! He got more poison and some ice cream for his wife and a little black satin ribbon for no reason at all. She smiled at his thoughtfulness and thanked him.

Needless to say, he became so caught up in his fascination with death the chicken yard was soon empty. They looked so funny as they danced around and cackled and then just keeled over! That was the problem, they died so fast! You had to poison several just to get a good look! They would twitch a little for awhile, but that wasn't enough.

Mrs. Gunioff was alarmed at the deaths and at a loss as to the reason because her husband always saw to things like that. She had no sittin hen now so she sent Mr. Gunioff to get one and set it away from the chicken house where she could watch things better.

Then the sheep began to disappear and she couldn't understand why he was not more upset about it. She took her pet sheep, a baby lamb, and moved it closer to the house so she could watch it too!

Mr. Gunioff bought the poison in bulk now and had quite a bit left when he buried his last sheep. Somehow, by this time, he was sick at the loss and his mind rested about a month. His wife wondered that he did not replace them, a few anyway, because they were expensive. But he did not.

After the month or so had passed, his craving to see the dance of death returned and the cow was his choice to go. They had no children left at home so they didn't need all that milk! She, the cow, was different dying; she was large and her poor, pitiful moans were almost human as she labored to die and when she did die, he felt small satisfaction. A cow wasn't much fun to watch, the big body moving slowly, in pain.

A week later, it was the horse. It should have hurt him, cause he loved that horse he had had so long. But his obsession made any regret brief, if at all. He watched the horse die with his legs kicking and his eyes rolling in fear as he looked to his master, his friend, for help. Gunioff didn't bury the horse. He was tired. He just covered it up and went to sit on the porch and stare off into space.

Mrs. Gunioff lamented and cried in distress at the happenings on the farm as he listened and watched her, saying nothing.

Sunday it was, yes, it was a Sunday. Mrs. Gunioff went off to church with the Conets in their wagon, wavin good-by to Mr. Gunioff. She spoke to them of how outdone he was by the loss of all his animals, poor fellow! He just didn't feel up to doing anything. They nodded in understanding and continued down the bumpy dirt road, with Mrs. Conet lookin round their yard, trying to find something they had that she didn't, so she could have something to complain to her husband about again. She thought Mr. Gunioff was a better man than her husband anyway.

After they had gone, Mr. Gunioff got into his wagon and rode to town and got some strawberry ice cream, yes, strawberry it was, and returned to wait for his wife and friends to return.

While he waited he fed the poison to the new sitting hen. For some reason he didn't want to kill the little chicks, even tho he was leaving them without a mother. She just gave a twitch or two and then fell over!

When Martha, that was his wife's first name, returned, he met the wagon and reached up to help her down. Mrs. Conet smiled down at him. Well, there wasn't hardly nobody else round this country to flirt with. Anyway, that smile made him say, "I went and got you some ice cream for a treat, Martha."

"Ohhhhhh," Martha sang, "how nice! I sure would love some ice cream."

He smiled up at Mrs. Conet. "Strawberry. Would you like some too?"

Mr. Conet spoke, "Mama made me and Mavis (that was his wife's first name) a fine chocolate cake, going to save myself for that. Sure thank you tho!"

Mavis smiled down at Mr. Gunioff. "Thank you so much." She said softly, eyes glowin at him.

As they drove down the drive, Mavis looked back to watch Martha and her sweet husband go into their house, arms around each other. She smiled at the thought of love, lasting love. . . . Then she turned to her husband and frowned.

When Mr. Gunioff went through the front door, he said, "You just sit on the porch and rest yourself! I'll fix it for you for a change!" Martha sat with a big smile on her face, thinking how time can bring about a change and what a good one this was. Why, she and Mr. Gunioff may have a sweet full life ahead of them yet! With a little fun in it!

He mixed the ice cream and the poison and put it in one of her prettiest dishes she always saved for special times and took it to her. As she took the dish, she smiled and asked, "Where's yours? Ain't you goin to have some?"

"Goin to get it now," he said. And did. When he returned, he held his dish and watched her, smiling as she ate and licked her spoon.

All of a sudden, in the middle of tellin him about her day

at church, she grabbed her stomach and stared at him. Even in her pain, thoughts flooded into her mind and she realized what he had done to the animals and to her. She was pointing at the sheep yard when her body lurched and she was thrown on the floor of the porch. Her body shuddered and lurched again, with a life, or a death, of its own, and she flew off the porch to the ground. Through her pain, she saw him moving closer to her, she looked at him, when her head wasn't jerkin with eyes rollin up, in wonder. He had sat his bowl down. He was crying. He cried until she died, looking at her with a deep sadness. She never did scream, just struggled with the monster in her mind and in her body and in her sight. She forgot to pray, she was tryin so hard to understand this man she had lived with, loved, most all her life. Then . . . her heart lost the struggle . . . and she died.

Mr. Gunioff went into the house and brought out a large mirror, setting it in front of him, he began to eat his ice cream. He was staring at himself as the tremors began. His arm flung the dish away involuntarily, but he had eaten enough. He looked at himself, when he could, through the pain and the contortions of his body. He did not understand how he got there in the middle of all this death.

Just as he was closing his eyes for the last time, the little sheep that belonged to his wife came bouncing around the house from the sheltered field. Mr. Gunioff's last smile was for life. He was glad he had missed the little sheep.

By that time, as the Millers rounded the curve going into their own driveway, they heard the bleating of the little sheep at the Gunioff's, faintly.

Mavis turned angrily to her husband. Said, "You don't never do nothin like that for me! He thinks of her and makes her know he loves her! You ain't never brought me no ice cream in a long time! They over there right now, just as happy, eating that ice cream."

Mr. Conet spoke, softly, "Mavis, that ain't true. You always lookin at what you think is greener grass. I love you and I bring you things. We just now lately got you that pretty suit you got on today."

Mavis threw her head up. "Humph! Cause I let you make love to me! That's all you ever want to do! is make love!

You hear that? That chile say all he wants to do is make love!

Now . . . I can't blame her for not knowin zackly what is happenin over at her neighbors. But I can blame her for not knowin zackly enough bout life to know when she is well off!

Well, now. It's plenty more sayings could go with this story, but I'll just let it speak for itself. Cause I been lookin at my own grass lately and it sure could use some of my attention. I want my grass to be green, green. Evergreen! Just in case.

FRIENDS, ANYONE?

You know, I am a grown woman of some considerable character and an excellent education. Which age, I am not going to tell you. I mean, how important is age? Just try to live, I say, with wisdom and concern for others. But, by living this long (not too long), I have learned a few things.

Everybody remembers their mother talking about friends. How few you have no matter how long you live? That is what I wish to speak about. I have really been fooled, so I know from whence I speak. Let me explain.

I was born and grew up in a little township that no longer exists. An octopus city has reached out, surrounded and devoured it, luckily. I guess there were about 700 fairly normal people living there then.

As to friends, I was born about the same time and grew up with my friend, Jana Green. Our mothers were good friends until the day my mother heard me screaming where I lay with my friend, Jana, in a crib. My mother came in to discover my entire cheek in Jana's mouth. The teeth marks remained two days! Attacked! . . . and I was only a baby!

I remember the look of hatred my mother gave to Jana's mother and Jana. Jana's mother picked her up and held her to her breast as if to protect her from my mother. Nothing came of it, except Jana and her mother soon left and did not soon come back. We didn't go to their house again soon either.

Over the years that was forgotten and our little friendship grew. We did everything together. Learned together about life. Learned to swim in the creek, fish, went to school, hated the same teachers, loved the same teachers, sometimes. Had separate birthday parties because I think my mother still didn't trust, nor like, Jana. We had the whooping cough and measles together, everything. We were very close, even if we were different kinds of people. Well . . . you know children.

Her mother and father were said to be good-looking. Brown with brown eyes. Jana had ugly gold glints in her full head of auburn hair and unseemly light-brown eyes. I was also brown, as were my mother and father, but the sunlight was not in our brown, which is better, I think, personally. My hair didn't glint, but I think that is the sign of a lady, personally.

Jana's body was matured, full and rounded, rather vulgar I might say. While I stayed thin, because thin is better. Her teeth were even, while I had to wear braces. But this finally gave me better looking teeth. Her feet were small because she liked shoes, not bare feet. Now, my feet were large. I liked bare feet, not shoes, to be close to nature and natural, the best, I might say. Also, my mother was too dumb to warn me. Jana liked to laugh a lot, I remember. I was quiet, thoughtful, like somebody with some sense.

These small differences made us no never-mind at that time. My lord! We were children, friends, and played as such. I was a very innocent, fair-minded child and would never have felt an ugly inclination anyway.

I remember one day, we were playing with some boys and they devised a game whereby the girls ran and if they were caught by the boys, the boys could kiss them! I think Jana thought of that game, she was always ahead of all the other girls and liked boys early. Too early I might say.

Of course, all the girls ran! And, going along with Jana as usual, I ran. I remember feeling my chest grow warm with my excited and accelerated breath. My legs feeling the exhileration of running and my smiles when I looked back to see who was gaining on whom.

My excitement fell flat. There was no boy there behind me! No one had run after me! Well, of course, I was innocent in mind and body, they probably knew that. But still . . . no boy had run after me. Me! All the girls were caught and screaming, playfully struggling to be let loose. Even Jana. She could sure fool people. The worse thing was, all the extra boys were sitting around on the grass! Doing nothing! Not even looking my way.

I walked back with dignity and sat down on the grass

too, and just looked at the caught girls. Then Jana came over and put her arms around me and kissed me on my cheek. The one she had bitten years ago. Well, that passed, thank God.

But . . . other things I didn't understand. Jana always got valentine cards, boxes of candy, flowers, as we got older. Even little scraggly ones when we were young, that some boy had stolen, no doubt. She never missed a graduation party once we were in high school. Not one! The boys always asked her. I wondered why, but in my innocence, what could I even guess? My mother said not to worry about these things. That one day Jana would come up with a baby from all that company and going all the time. Then we would see what was what!

So . . . I studied hard in school. Made good . . . kinda good grades. What else was there to do?

Now, there was one boy, young man, I should say. Albert, who always took me wherever I had to go with someone and I always went with him wherever he had to go with someone. I guess you could say he was not good-looking. He was small and wiry . . . but smart. I thought I hated him. Anyway, I used to feel like I did. He was just a hometown boy we had grown up with.

High school graduation was near, and going on to college, for some. When a young man by name of Nathan moved to our town with his family. He was truly blessed. Good-looking, tall, strong, handsome and his family had money!

They lived in a small house, like the usual in our town, while they built a larger one. And do you know . . . before that house was finished being built, he suffered tragedy. His father had died from something. His mother was sick, maybe dying. And he was in love with Jana . . . and they were planning to be married. Yes, mam.

That friend of mine didn't care what was happening to that poor man, she was only thinking of herself! Marriage! I knew her family was poor and she might not be able to get to college, but for heavens sake! Thinking of marriage in the midst of all Nathan's problems! Well, some people are like that, think of nobody but themselves.

Well, since it seemed like the thing to do and I couldn't let her outdo me by getting engaged first, Albert and I became engaged. He had already gone off to college to study law. I was soon to leave for college myself. Jana was supposed to be trying to get a grant or something to go to college herself, but she was so in loooove with Nathan. He had to stay home and take care of the property and his mother. Jana decided to give it all up for him . . . and loooove. I told her she was a fool to do that! She better get her education. She might need it. She would need it! What could she do in this little one-horse town with no greater education? Nothing! Honey, this is only a place to leave! How dumb could she be?!

Now, just between me and you, I was even kind of sure Nathan didn't love her. Wellll, I can't tell you everything, it's not good to tell everything. But . . . one day . . . Nathan made love to ME! It cost me a lot in pride and things like that, but I just had to know how it would feel to be in his arms. And, also, if he really was going to be true to my friend, Jana. Well, when it was over, I didn't like him one bit! Not one bit! He didn't treat me like a lady! He acted like

I was a tramp! Like he didn't love me one bit! I left him alone after that, I showed him he didn't mean nothing to me.

Then, horror of horrors, I soon found I was pregnant! And it was not Albert's child! We didn't have abortions then, not like now. All my new, best friends have had them, two or three times. But my friends are grown women, college graduates. I was just a child then, you might say.

I tried all the home remedies I could find and when nothing worked, my mother locked me in my room and told everyone I was gone away to college early. Except Jana. Because Jana helped me with my schoolwork to keep up and stay ready for college and, of course, I needed someone to talk to, keep me company in that little dark room for seven months! I had no other friends at that time.

Jana told Albert I was sick when he called. Because, you see, it wasn't his child. Jana helped to care for me, out of some goodness she found in her heart, and I was delivered at home by a family friend—doctor.

Oh! My friend, listen to me. Fate has ever and always been unkind to me. Maybe if I had had one child I could struggle courageously under that burden. But Fate had other plans. I had twins! Twins! Dear lord, one was blind, the other deaf! Two girls. Born to me, an innocent, loving, unsuspecting person. Ignorant of life.

Now, as a mother, I'm sure I didn't hate them. How can a mother hate her children? But I did not love them. Look what they had cost me! I had dreamed of showing Nathan, yes, Nathan, "his" love child, his son! Now I never could. The poor man would never know about these blind and deaf babies. Not if I had to tell him!

My mother had a friend who had recently lost her bastard child, she gave the twins to this wayward friend, of all people!, to keep for awhile. They made some agreement. I couldn't be worried at that time, I had to prepare for my future. College.

I was soon on my way to college. Waving good-by gaily from the train window to Jana and my mother. Good-by to this stupid, stupid town and all the stupid, cold-hearted people in it. Good-by at last. It was their loss, it sure wasn't mine. I had greater things to do, to be. I looked back at Jana standing there beside my mother. I smiled. Because one of us had made it, you see? Take my word, it was the right one.

I became so involved in my life at college, I soon forgot my hometown except for hurried calls to my mother when I needed money. Isn't it strange how people don't realize how you need money when you are away? I mean, why did she wait until I called? She wasn't that broke! She didn't need to keep making all her bills, if she knew I was away and needed money! I was her child! Her real responsibility! My mother always was just a little dumb. She didn't have anything else to do and I had all that college work!

But there was a good side to all this. I grew lovely as I grew older. I did very well with the college men and my social life. I knew now you had to offer them something. I did very well academically too! Much to my regret, I didn't have good clothes. My mother said she had to help with the twins. Huh! Why didn't that woman, what's her name whose bastard died, who was keeping them, spend some of her own money on them? Hell, she was getting all the pleasure! But all that was soon to change.

Time passed, Albert graduated and was in demand he was so excellent at law. I could have graduated, but I liked going to college so much, I kept finding excuses and reasons to remain. My mother complained about the money, but I was her child, only child, except for those grandchildren she was always writing me about. I use to burn the letters. She should have known better! Someone might have seen them.

Albert's confidence had helped improve his looks and carriage, not much, but enough to count. Our future looked good. He had paid more attention to his books than to the girls where he was, so he still wanted to marry me. He didn't fool me tho, I knew they hadn't paid any attention to him.

We came home to be married.

Naturally, first thing I did was go see my friend Jana. She certainly looked overworked and tired. She had a brow-beaten son, I guess that was why he was so well-behaved. Imagine, she still did all her own housework and had to care for her mother-in-law and the family business too! I had thought she had some sense. People sure can fool you, let you down.

Nathan was, maybe, fooling around doing everything except what he should have been doing, which was running the business his father left him. The business was going down except for the work Jana put into it. While we were in town, Albert, my husband, went over and helped her straighten out her books and things. He even gave her some new ideas to work on. She almost cried she was so grateful! I was very happy about that because I remember when she wouldn't have looked twice at Albert. You see, it pays to be humble.

Our wedding was rather grand, if I do say so myself! Jana was there, but she looked kind of dowdy, if you ask me. When Nathan got drunk at the reception and started hugging on the ladies, she left with her son.

Oh! The twins! I had forgotten. I didn't get a chance to go see them. To be truthful, I didn't want to ruin everyone's happiness. It made me so sad to think of them, blind and deaf. So . . . I left them in peace. It broke my heart.

After a brief honeymoon, we went East to live. Albert said we really could not afford a honeymoon at that time nor money, but I insisted. After all, you're only married once and Fate had been so unkind to me in the past, I needed all the little happiness I am due.

Albert went to work in a fabulous office making fabulous money. Soon, well, two or three years, I had a fabulous house and two cars and a lovely mink coat! Albert was doing so well! The friends I chose were all doing well also. They had married well, like I had, or they were college graduates doing well, like I was. I had my degree in human psychology. I had Friends of my stature, of course.

I worked so I could entertain, buy more clothes, since he fussed so about "squandering" money. He was always saying things like "Suppose something happens to the economy? What about the future?" You know? Just bull-shit! Pardon me. But I was living my future I had dreamed of like I had some sense!

I liked my shape and my clothes, so no babies for me. Besides I already knew about all that baby shit. Pain, honey, pain, everlasting.

Oh! The twins! Well, they were doing alright, I guess. The lady with the bastard child that died had died too. My mother couldn't take on all that work, so Jana was taking them over for her. For me, I guess. There must have been some money in it for her, but, with my generous soul, I prefer to think it was because she was my good friend and loved me. Actually, she had only taken Nathan's children, whether she knew it or not. It was his responsibility, so it really wasn't a favor to me!

The twins were almost eleven years old now, so they must be a lot of help at that age. I know Jana must have had some benefits from that. Besides Albert was helping her, now and then, with their business. Free. I wondered about that sometime, but I didn't worry. I just figured she owed me. Albert said the business was doing quite well. You know you have to pay in some way for that kind of assistance.

Anyway, life went on and I went on. Albert kept pestering me for children. But I didn't really want him so I sure didn't want his, or any, children. I was having the time of my life! This life was what I had struggled for, worked for, lived for, dreamed of and planned to keep!

I lunched and dined with my friends, everyday. Wore the finest clothes, drove the best cars, drank the best liquor, met the FINEST MEN! Some of them belonged to my friends, but they didn't seem to mind if they "strayed" because my friends were straying themselves. But, we kept it in the "circle" and that's the best way, don't you think? Some of my friends had their tubes tied, to avoid the "terrible responsibility" meant only for the dumbest, uneducated women. I had mine tied also. I NEVER told Albert. Goodness, no! He would have died. He wanted a "family." Aren't some people futile?

Then . . . my mother had to go and die on me. I had tried to make her come visit me. She wouldn't. I don't know why. My house was much better than hers. I didn't like to go there. Just tell me, why should I when she could come to me?

I used to have to go home with Albert when he went home to "rest," he said. I would see Mama then, but I just can't stand that tiny-ass place! They didn't even have a decent cocktail lounge! And no liquor stores in town. No country club, no friends to play bridge with. You could go insane! I always returned to the city early and left him there in the country. Country! Cemetery, I called it.

Anyway, when Mama died, I just HAD to go home then. I was heart-broken. Fate is so cruel to me. My own mother! Jana's mother was still living, tho her mother-in-law had passed on. She had all the luck.

During the funeral Jana cried so hard, I said, "My God, it's MY mother! No need for a show." After the funeral, I didn't feel like staying in that little ole ugly house, so I went to see Jana out of boredom. We hadn't talked much at the funeral. She was always moving away. Didn't want to stand beside me, cause I was looking gorgeous. City elegance! Natural only to a select few.

I have to say that big ole house she lived in was really comfortable for a country-type house. You understand what I mean? I prefer elegance and luxury, but Jana's home was quite sufficient for the country. She served vodka and orange juice. I asked her if she had tried champagne and orange juice. She hadn't! See what I mean?

She still had that ugly auburn hair and those ugly light-brown eyes. Her figure was still decent. She looked well, but she didn't know the first thing about dressing. I had worn my full-length mink coat over my black Chanel dress, and now I was sorry because it made her look so . . . so dowdy. So cheap . . . so nothing. You know?

We talked awhile, well, I did all the talking about my

friends, my home and all the exciting things I do. Trying to enlighten her, liven up her life. She actually interrupted to ask me, "Are you planning to take the twins?"

My sense of decency was outraged! I gasped, "Oh! No! How could I uproot them? That wouldn't be showing love. How could you suggest such a thing, Jana?" She was a cold-blooded bitch to suggest such a thing!

She leaned back in that old chair, said, "Then I want to adopt them legally. After all . . . they are Nathan's also." It was so gross, uncouth, for her to say that to my face. Me! Her friend!

I gasped again, I couldn't help it. The audacity! I told her, too. "Who told you that?!" Had she no shame? "How dare you say such a thing to me, a friend!" I knew my mother did not betray me to this . . . this insensitive bitch!

She waved her hand at ME, as if I were a fly. "Your mother did first, then Nathan admitted they could be his. And . . . they look just like him."

I rose from my seat, sat my glass down and knelt before her, forgetting myself always. "Let me explain. I meant you no harm."

Jana moved slightly away from me. I thought to myself, "Look at this bitch! I'm her friend since school days. My mother just died even. And she moved away from ME?"

She said, "You don't have to explain. The twins are explanation enough. I love them and I want to adopt them."

Now, when she said she loved them, I wondered what she knew that I didn't. Was Nathan leaving them a great deal of money? Had I missed something? But thinking evil gives me a headache. That's why I never do it. I decided to think about it later. I said, still on my knees, "I don't want Albert to know!"

She was silent and I don't like people to be silent around me. I continued, saying, "Albert may be a lawyer, but he cannot handle the adoption. You'll have to pay someone else for that!"

She smiled, sadly, "It does not matter. He is handling my divorce, that's enough. He can refer me to someone else for the adoption."

I started thinking, trying to understand what was happening. After all, I do have a degree in human psychology! I remember asking, "Your divorce? You? You are leaving Nathan?!"

She had no life in her at all. Said, "What difference does it make to you?"

I was speechless, until it occurred to me to ask, "You are going to give up this house? The business?"

In a dead, lifeless tone, she answered, "What difference does it make?"

Then, speechless again for a moment, thinking of how my dear mother was now gone and what would I do if she forced those disabled twins on me. I asked, "You still want to adopt the kids? A deaf and blind set of twins?"

I understand, now, she cannot face truths, facts. She answered me, "They are whole, fine young ladies!"

I thought to myself, "Lord, it takes all kinds! Thank the Lord, I am not a fool!" I finished my drink. Forgot it was as hot as it was outside, so I threw on my mink coat. I wondered, out loud, "Where are they, the twins?"

She stood. "At the library," she said.

I turned to go, smiling at my thought. "The blind one also?"

I could have sworn I heard disgust in her voice. "They have braille at the library . . . and friends." She seemed annoyed.

My eyes misted, I turned back to her, asked, "Do they ever wonder who their mother really is?" After all, I am a real mother!

The answer came, "They know who their mother is."

I whispered, lest someone was in the house with us. "You mean you?"

She finished her drink. Said, "I mean you."

I must have looked strange, I should have. I was strangling!

She stepped close to me, looking directly into my eyes. I hate people to do that to me.

She said, "Don't you know your mother loved those children? She loved them! She was their grandmother! They were the only grandchildren she ever had, ever would have."

I was suffocating . . . I had to leave. I wanted another drink, but I had something at my mother's house, or in the car. I opened the door to leave and was going down the front steps, when she called to me.

"Nona?"

I turned, waiting, wishing her to hurry and say whatever it was. I knew she probably wanted to get me to let her visit me after her divorce. I wondered how I could say no. I didn't want to be bothered with her! She would never fit in my crowd. We were ladies in the truest sense.

"Nona, when the adoption is over, don't come where I am or the girls are, ever again, while I am alive."

I couldn't believe my ears. This country-nothing bitch talking to me like that! "Just what do you mean?" I demanded.

Very quietly, calmly, this woman said to me, "You are a waste of time. My time, their time and God's time." Then, in my face! That bitch closed the door!

Well! A lady of my sensibilities and sensitivities, I couldn't take it. I walked away bewildered, understanding nothing of this type of person, even with my education. I had never really known her at all. She was never my friend at all. Why does Fate choose me for these horrible things?

Then . . . almost to my Mercedes, where I am longing to take that hot coat off . . . I see them! My children, my twins, coming toward me. Me, their real mother. Their arms were loaded with books, while they each held a hand of Jana's young son. They were laughing and talking in ladylike tones. Not shouting like some kids do in the street. I knew they had inherited their ladylike ways from me. I looked at their clothes, as a mother should, to see if Jana was treating them as good as she treated her son. They were neat in bright sweaters and pleated skirts, white oxfords and brown moccasins. Long, beautiful braids were wrapped around their heads. They were beautiful! My children.

Now! I knew why she wanted them! . . . and I wanted them too! That woman could not talk to me like that and get away with it! And my precious babies too?! This is ME!

I walk toward them, my lovely daughters, I hold out my hand to one, I speak to both. I smile at them. I do not remember their names or who is who. I do not know which one can see, which can hear. But, oh, their beauty is mine. My heart is full.

One looks, one turns her head toward me, their mother, as if I am a stranger. They pass me by. Me . . . their real mother, passed by! Oh, that hurt. But I began to understand. My education, you know? Perhaps they didn't mean to. I rather think that the one I spoke to was the one who cannot hear. The one I held my hand out to, smiled at, was the one who cannot see. I watched them move away from me, a broken woman. I had to get away from there. I needed a drink.

I reached the house where my mother lived, my house now. Albert needn't think he will get his hands on that! I had had all I could stand for one day! I fix myself a drink and just sit in that dingy little house my mother had lived in so long, thinking of what life gives me to deal with. Then . . . Albert comes in from somewhere. He's been so busy running around this place he loves so much, I had forgotten him. As usual.

He looked at my drink in my hand and frowned. He thinks I drink too much. I almost told him I had to drink to stand him and his boring life. Work, work, work. So stupid. Anyway, I don't feel like talking to a fool just then.

He talked anyway. "Nona? I am taking steps to move my law practice back here at home."

I looked at him like he was crazy. I told him so. "Here!? Albert, we're not moving back here. I can not possibly live in this dead, empty place. All my friends are in the East. I have nothing here and no one here any longer. I will not return here to live."

The man calmly told me, "That won't be necessary. That won't be necessary at all. Ever."

Incredulous, I asked, "What do you mean? We are going

to live in two places? That is no marriage!" See, I needed him when I accepted certain invitations from professional people that came directly to him.

Still calm, he said to me, "It has not been a real marriage almost from the beginning, Nona. You do not love me. I've known that for a long, long time. And . . . quite honestly . . . I do not love you any longer. I've tried, but I just can't seem to find something, anything, to love in you."

I shouted at him. "What are you talking about? You are my husband! I am your wife! Of course you love me!"

Still insufferably calm, he answered me, "You can find another husband. You need one who likes going to empty affairs, likes gossip, phony fronts, adultery, lies and . . . all the things you like, Nona."

I screamed at him, "You don't know anything about me! That's not true! Some no-good busybody person has lied to you . . . and you let them! I've made a good home, a good marriage for you. I've given you your best connections for your business! I've . . ."

He raised his hand to stop my words. "I don't even want to hear anything about what you've done or anything you have to say. Lies, all lies. I don't want to fight with you. I just want a divorce. I'll take care of everything. As usual."

I tried to stop shouting, "I know damn well you will! You are going to PAY for doing a horrible thing like this to ME!"

He got up to end the conversation. "I know what I will pay. I've already taken care of that. Keep the house. Keep your car. Keep your life. But you cannot keep me." He turned and walked away and out of the house. Out of the beautiful life I had made for him. Why, he was nothing without me!

I shouted after him, crying. "My mother just died. How can you do such a thing to me on this day? You never have given a thought to how I feel." He never did turn around. He was a selfish, unfeeling man. How had I missed seeing that in him? Some things must not be in psychology books!

I stood there a moment, trying to get a hold on my life. These people! Where did they come from? Don't they have any feelings? For me? Today I buried my mother. I have lost my children to an evil bitch of a woman. I truly have to lose them now if Albert's really gone, because I will not pay a lawyer all that money it would take to get them. I will have bills to pay as it is. I am losing my husband because he does not understand me. Does not realize all I have given up for him. All this has happened to me in one evil day.

My glass was empty. I filled it again. Lord knows, I truly needed a drink. I hoped I had brought enough with me to last me til I get home. I do not drink excessively. I am a lady of class and education and distinction. I have just had a hard, hard day. That's the reason I needed a drink!

Oh! Home, home. I was so glad to get home. I thought Albert would call or come back when he missed me. I'd un-tie my tubes, have a baby to hold him. I did not want a divorce. They don't like single women in my crowd. They always said "Her husband is a lawyer" when they intro-duced me without him there. So proud, my friends. That's what makes me wonder who the gossip was. Who told him all those vicious lies? Someone jealous, I bet. Someone whose husband liked me. Someone who resented my looks, my clothes.

Albert did everything but call. He moved, but commuted to work in both offices. I got the house, my Mercedes, some rental property. But, now, I HAVE to work. Support myself. I tried to get Albert back, but he didn't have sense enough to know he was trading a Doctor and the high life-style for a cemetery. Didn't know what he was losing.

I decided to think of all I was gaining. Freedom to be me. Myself. At first it was fun. I invested some of my money in a new wardrobe, because I had to attract new men. A husband. Someone to take care of me I could be proud of when I went out with him at my side. I did look ever so good, I must say. Gorgeous.

But, people are so selfish, so chicken-shit. Some of the women I thought were my BEST friends began to be too busy to see me anymore. I used to have to search around to find someone of stature to have lunch with everyday. Those used to be the best gossip sessions! Now I bet they are talking about me when they get together. Because I am free and able to do whatever I want to. Jealous! I know they are!

A few of the men I use to see when I was married . . . they came around for awhile. But I know my value, so I quit calling them because I don't have to beg. One of them was very close to me at one time, too. Reginal. I love that name. So aristocratic. I thought perhaps, if I got pregnant by him, he would marry me. He wasn't much, just a city coordinator or something like that. Nothing special to make anyone take notice or be jealous. Still, he would be a husband! When I did, secretly, un-tie my tubes, I did get pregnant.

I thought it was a good idea to have a child. It seemed like children had been a help to Jana getting a man. When I told Reginal about the gift I was about to give him, he said it was a good thing I had a degree so I could take care of a baby, because he couldn't help me. Said he didn't even know

65

if it was his! What did he think I was!? He said he had other plans and marriage wasn't in them. Can you imagine that? A city coordinator with a chance to marry a Social Psychologist, a Doctor, saying it was not in his plans? That's why he isn't anything! He has no sense of getting ahead in life! I left him alone right then. I had to . . . remove that baby too. A single woman can't be so encumbered. I never would get a man with a baby laying, slobbering, in my arms.

Besides I plan to get my own children back when they are grown and can appreciate me.

But listen! Jana did it again! I was hearing rumors when I had to go home to see about that property of mine. It seems Jana and Albert are together pretty steady. He is even investing in a business for her! Her divorce is final and she is the marrying type. The slick kind of woman that sets a scheme and makes it work. I know her! I, also, know Albert is the marrying kind. When he likes a woman, he sticks to her. Why he ever got a divorce from me, I'll never know. I complemented his role in life. Probably some lies Jana told him because she wanted him for herself. I hear he deluges her with flowers, candy and gifts. Many gifts. Why? He never did that for me! She probably tricks him in some way for that!

But, times change and I know things will get better as soon as I meet more people and they find out who I am and what kind of person I am. I do have a degree in psychology. A Doctorate!

I go out, now, with a few ordinary working women sometimes. They are nothing much. Just company sometimes, when they are not going out with their "ordinary men." I simply cannot go out with just an ordinary man, that is beneath me. I just can't. I won't! I deserve more.

I can't understand what is wrong! Is it the times?

The men don't come.

My mother is dead. I don't have anyone.

I get along, tho. I am a smart, modern woman. However . . . I am just a little tired of being pawed by one-night stands. If you go all the way, you never know if it will be good or not! It is mostly not! Further, most of them do not have the decency to call back. They eat your food, listen to your music, drink all your liquor, ask you to do all kinds of things. Then, you never hear from them again.

It galls me when I hear how good Albert is to Jana. He never was to me! I hear they may marry. Two fools, maybe they deserve each other.

I know one thing, tho. I am smart, I have a degree and I am gorgeous. I will find another man who is somebody bigger than Albert! There is someone out there who will love me, marry me.

God forbid, I may have to be alone. Awhile.

You know . . . Fate has ever been unkind to me. Always . . . cruel and unkind. People like I am, are always done this way. Fate is so unfair to us. To me.

LATER: ALONE

The little lady had paid for an invitation to this swank affair. She pulled her slightly worn-looking mink coat closer around her, even in the sweltering heat of the day. She looked gorgeous. Inside the grand room prepared for a luncheon she lifted a drink from a tray, moved toward a table with her name on it, looked over the crowd to see which man was looking at her. None at the moment. She sat down, in her elegant practiced way . . . to think about her presence, her future and her hair. Thought many evil thoughts because people never did her right. Cried inside her mind because people never did her right.

Soon . . . others like her joined her. Both men and women. Both with too much makeup, to cover puffy, alcoholic or drug-abused faces. They drank together, but seldom looked at each other unless along with a snide remark. Their faces were turned away from their own table toward the rest of the crowded, busy room. Looking. Seeking.

All each alone, even together.

She never misses these things because she does not want to be a waste of time, nor does she want to waste time. Time is passing fast. It's precious.

She seldom mentions "Husband" any longer.

She says, "I just want a friend. A true friend at last! Is that too much to ask?" Everywhere she goes, her little, empty, hurt eyes ask, "Friends, anyone?"

I do not know how she came out in her pursuit of what she was after. I did not have the time to waste.

VANITY

I'm sittin here thinking, ponderin, over life. I hear my radio playin music softly round me. Beautiful full religious music bout God and what he does. I am listenin . . . and I am thinkin . . . about this life. Even death.

Sometimes you get something in life and you don't know you got it, so you don't do nothin with it. Then sometime you get something and you know you got it and you want everybody else to know it too. You be just done got lucky, even got something you can share, like beauty. But some people turn a gift into a weapon and use it on everybody. Sometimes, they think they be goin up, up . . . but they ain't. They be goin down, down . . . and taking people with em!

Two fools. Fool for doin it, and a fool for goin down with it. One thing I do know, life is like a bank sometime. You ain't gonna get no more out of it than you put in it! Tho it do look like some people do . . . in the end, they don't.

Some people say everybody got a Guardian Angel looks over you. I ain't sure God got that kind of labor to waste on some people, but if he do, I don't envy the one was watchin over Vanity.

My mind is turned to these thoughts by death. A strange death, ugh!, of a woman I knew. A friend? I don't know was she a friend or not. She might'a tried, I don't know. I was her friend tho. I do know that. Vanity. Vanity is her name.

I knew her well. Very well. I am a little older than she was. I used to keep her, sit with her for her mama when Vanity was little. She was grown then, in a little way. She talk to me all her life. She thought I was her friend . . . well I was, but I was a little scared of her. I was. She didn't seem to have nothin in her heart for nobody but herself. I watched her think, listened to her talk.

Just listen what she said to me a year or so ago, when her trouble started. Another kind of trouble she didn't understand. See, she didn't have no women friends for too long. They didn't like her for long. But she never cared noway. She get lonely she just come find me. I knew all her secrets. I think. Just listen what she said to me when we be sittin on the front porch, laughin, talkin softly. She be drinkin champagne. She drink enough to keep even a Guardian Angel high.

She say, "I was always very beautiful. You may not believe that, but it's true. I know. I am still beautiful.

"I knew I was beautiful the day I was born. You may not

believe that either, that a newborn could know that, but I did. The doctor did not want to slap me, the nurses looked at me with envy and hate. My mother was elated. She was . . . uncomely. But I let that pass. ME. I was the important one . . . and . . . as I said I was beautiful. But bored . . . from birth.

"Bored! Do you know how long I had to wait to walk? To speak? To buy things, beautiful clothes, to enhance my beauty? Several years. But I used the time well.

"I studied my father. I wrapped his heart around all my fingers. Many times he slept, holding me, instead of my mother. That became a problem, but I don't wish to talk about that now. But . . . I was practicing, yes, practicing for my future. When I spoke, I spoke in question marks. 'Will you buy that for me? May I have that? Do you think this is right for me? Don't you want me to have that? Does this look good on me, compliment me?' Oh yes, I knew what to do with me, my beauty.

"I wanted to goooo somewhere. Beeee somebody. Doooo something with what I had. I was born decided not to be a victim. Determined. And I had the greatest tool I know in life. Beauty.

"At five, ten, twelve, fifteen years of age, I knew, I knew, just by looking at people looking at me. I knew I was superb . . . that I could acquire things and people in proportion to my beauty. The world lets you know they are fools because they love beauty no matter how empty it is. However, I was not empty. I was full of thoughts. Of myself. Well . . . what better? Who should you be thinking of? See?" She said and laughed, "I'm still into question marks?

"Reasons, causes and effects, results . . . that's what I

studied on. Hard. But not too hard . . . it wasn't necessary . . . for all. Boys and then men became monotonous, always telling me of their love. What did they think I thought? Didn't I know they would love me? Want me? I was delicious to look upon. Ask my father. He gave me everything! He loved to touch me, assure himself I was his. My mother had very little, she didn't need it anyway. She had her chosen man . . . who really belonged to me after I was born. She had us. She had him anyway. I was there I guess. But only I had me.

"Many, many hours were spent, me with myself, alone. The sun rose and shone on ME, sent its warmth into my soul. Flowers bent when I passed, God knew. Everyone, anyone, who looked on me, their heart beat and throbbed with the thoughts of love and possession. Men and some women too. Desire . . . ahhhh, desire, the crux of the whole life matter.

"I was young . . . innocent, in a way, in my body, not my mind. I was sad because I had to wait for life, get older. Wait for the joy of being a woman. A beautiful woman. To get my due. I said prayers. After all, God was, is, greater than I, at least." (I know her Guardian Angel almost choked!)

"So many loves came into my life, before my eyes. I was always smiling, happy. At peace with my self and my glory. I cared, oh!, I cared for myself because when I first looked at me, I loved, loved me.

"At twelve years old, I washed, creamed and smoothed my body. I brushed, combed my luxuriant hair that it might nestle on my lovely soft shoulders and be a cape of beauty for others to enjoy. Yes, I thought of others, sometime. I loved my arms, my waist, my legs, so full and smooth, beautiful . . . and mine.

"You know I loved clothes! To sheath my body! Let them be expensive! Let my father struggle to do what he had to do to afford them for me. Wasn't I his child? Wasn't he supposed to do for me? Getting anything I needed? I needed beauty. As I grew older, I HAD to have lovely, beautiful, costly things. Wasn't I ME!? Mama had had her time and got him . . . and me . . . now it was my turn. Practicing, practicing. My hands, my nails, my shoulders, my breast, beautiful. My legs, my thighs, my feet . . . all of me, I oiled, creamed, smoothed and loved. And I felt joy. Anything that made me look like me . . . beautiful . . . I loved. Not people . . . just things.

"The only thing that bothered me was time. TIME. Always moving, passing, getting away. But too slow for me. I had to wait, wait and waste those early years I needed, to be admired and loved. I got up early, mornings, to have more time to be admired. I have sat looking out my windows, hours and hours, weeks and weeks, just waiting for someone new to come along, pass by, to look upon me and know . . . I was beautiful. I watched their eyes.

"Seasons meant nothing to me. All were mine. Except, I learned I must stay out of the sun. Ahhh, and it was such a spotlight.

"One day after school graduation, after all the shit I had to go through to get to my life, my freedom, I said to myself, 'I'm not beautiful enough.' You see, I had seen others then, that might come close to me. And I wished, tho I looked better than all others, that all, ALL pretty women, even cute women, would die, DIE. And leave me to have all the men, all the adulation, my choice, anybody I wanted . . . to love me.

"Somebody special to love me. It was now at the time when loving myself was not enough . . . not enough. I began to know fear. Fear is a low, low, sad feeling. But it was into me. I couldn't help it. Of course, I should have known better. What had fear to do with me? YET . . . I feared. Somehow I knew . . . I might not . . . might not . . . have everything. Oh! my lord, ME!?

"Now! It was now time. I was eighteen. Through with high school. My parents could not afford college where I might have found my true future, my love to love me as I should be loved. Riches, position, everything! No . . . I had to work with what I had. Welll, it was quite a bit. But, still, all by myself. Only, only?, my beauty to help me. And it did. Don't you make the mistake that men will not let anything go for a beautiful thing to look at. In the morning, the evening, especially the night. Men are fools. Good grand fools. Don't let me mislead you, they are alright. Are they not rich sometimes? I still believe the world belongs to a woman, but only because it belongs to men and they give it to her! Just fools for beauty. Is it beauty? Or is it body? Hmmmm. But . . . I was always just like a lady, a real lady. A beautiful, beautiful Lady."

Yessss, chile! All those things Vanity said to me . . . and more. I can't remember everything now, my mind is mixed up with death . . . and life.

I'ma tell you something, bout this life I done found out. Sometimes from the birthstone to the tombstone ain't nothing but a few steps. High ones, low ones. Don't matter. And sometime you don't even know you been walking on the road of time, think you been standin still and you been flyin with your feet. Laughin, having a good time, even cryin, having a bad time. Then, one day, you look up and you way, way up the road. One day you twenty, overnight, you thirty, one movin year . . . forty, one afternoon . . . fifty. After that, it pass by like hours, minutes! All the time you thought you was spending only money, you been spending time. TIME. Chile, time. The most valuable thing you got! Or ever gonna have!

Now, if you ain't there where you think you ought to be when you think you oughta be THERE, and you done spent time til you broke and you ain't even enjoyed gettin to where you are! If you don't understand what I'm sayin, I do, I just maybe ain't sayin it right for you to understand. Try.

There was no lie about it! Vanity was a beautiful thing, a beautiful woman to see. Not to know. Just to see. Her Guardian Angel had a JOB!

But, back to her family, her dear mother saw the love transferred away from her. She wasn't no longer the center of the home. She just waned and drifted to the background with the second daughter she had, Mega. The father often slept with Vanity cause she said she had bad dreams, holdin her, pettin her, kissin her. As she grew older, them kisses grew lower and lower until she was kissed by father all over her body. It was like a form of worship to her. If it is true some men had their own daughters way, way back there in them cavemen days without feelin shame nor fear, that is still in some men. I don't blive he went that far with her tho. Just fondles, touches. But she grew to expect, and get, the same thing from most all her men the rest of her life. Her Guardian Angel musta shuddered.

Then, when Mega was born the father expected to have another great beauty to show off. He smiled and waited. But, as she grew, her beauty was neat, plain, sweet. He might could'a grew to understand those was also wonderful things to love, but Vanity always movin between them, pullin on his arms when he played with Mega, wrappin herself round his head to shield his eyes from Mega. In time, he centered on Vanity again. The mother cried awhile, then smiled thru her tears and took Mega to herself. Mega grew up affectionate, patient, sweet and, I guess, just normally normal. The mother refused to have any more children. So they each had one!

But these things tells on a woman who loves her husband. She loved her husband, had dreamed of the perfect home. Her love grieved, her spirit grieved. She was alone in her home, in her marriage, in her life. She was a sad, sad heartbroken woman, whose daughter had stolen her husband, with a smile. A beautiful smile. A Guardian Angel grieved, I know.

In time, when Vanity was seventeen, Mega fifteen, the parents divorced. The mother could take no more, could not watch Mega's confusion no more. The family had been divided too often and too long by Vanity's demands on her father. The mother took Mega, naturally, and because I don't have time to tell just everything, I'll just tell you they did well. Mega had a normal life, I guess. She wondered, from time to time, about the family ways. She loved them all. She was patient with them all. Just like a real little lady. Her time passed that way, and she grew up strong in spite of all of them.

All this time Vanity was runnin after hearts . . . anybody's. Had great pleasure in takin the heart of a boy, or man, who seemed to love another girl, or woman. Even her closest friends' beaus. Of course she ended up with no friends! But Vanity didn't care, she was havin a good time. Just like a lady (she thought). And time passed. Don't it always.

Her father bought her everything. Sometime being late, very late, with payments for Mega. Vanity explained that away to him by saying she gave Mega all her cast-off clothing and things, that Mega didn't need as much right at that time of her life.

Also, at that time of Vanity's life, she was twenty or twenty-one then, dancin, laughin, always goin out, riding, playin. Life was gettin dull to her. Same old crowd, growing smaller. Some gettin married. Women shyin away from her. Men already been burnt by her, keepin a distance. No magic around for her to play with. She turned her lofty head to look over the horizon for fresh life and dreams. Her Guardian Angel was in dread.

Vanity loved picture shows. Lookin at one, one day, she decided she had always wanted to be a movie star. She knew she looked as good as those up on that screen. She prepared her father a good meal (in her gloves). Set a beautiful table, candles and all, just for her father and her. His eyes just sparkled, he was so proud of his daughter and happy she had decided to stay home with him an evenin. Vanity didn't waste no time tho, she just came right out and told him almost soon as he sat down to eat.

"Daddy, I need some money. I've made up my mind what I want to be, at last. I'm going to Los Angeles to seek my fame . . . and my fortune. I know I will be successful.

All they want is beauty! So . . . I am prepared." She laughed, he frowned, started to say something. She thought she anticipated him. "You always wanted me to be serious about something. Now, I'm ready."

He sighed. They argued awhile. He lost, again.

He said, as he sighed, "Well . . . if that's what you really want. I'll transfer my job . . . and we'll move."

She pursed her beautiful lips. "Noooo. I want to . . . I need to go alone. I'm over twenty-one now. I want to be on my own. Just send me some money. But I want to be alone." She thought of allll the men there. And Dad was gettin old and showing it. Ugly comin. She didn't like ugly.

He was hurt . . . and feared loneliness. "You'd leave me? You'd go alone? So far from me?"

She turned her beautiful lips down, and snapped, "What do you expect me to do? Be here under . . . with you the rest of my life?"

He stammered, "No . . . no . . . I . . . I thought . . ."

She stopped his thought. "Well, I am grown. I will go alone. You can't be with me forever! I have to have my own life! I am your daughter . . . NOT your wife." He groaned and twisted in his seat, dinner, candles forgotten. She continued. "You'll . . . you'll still have Mega . . . and Mama, if you can get her to leave her new husband and come back to you! But I . . ."

He bent his dumb head. "Your mother will never leave that man. He loves her . . . and Mega." He looked up suddenly, angry. "He better not be doing anything to my child!" He looked sad again. "Let me get a house there and we . . ."

She threw him a disdainful look. "Dad. I . . . am . . .

grown. I have to go alone." Her tone softened, "I have to see if I can make it on my own. So you will be proud of me. Just a little money to help me til I am rich and can make it on my own." She smiled brightly, beautifully. "Then I will send for you to come . . . visit me sometime."

Anyway . . . she got her way. Her Guardian Angel shook its head . . . and waited.

Vanity went to Los Angeles expecting to have heads and hearts rolling in the streets. Instead she found so many beautiful women everywhere she went to seek a job. Everywhere she walked, ate, sat, looked. She got nervous and was throwing up every night. Got sick even, but didn't get a job in films. Men had so much pretty to look upon. She was just one of them. Beauty was five feet deep in Los Angeles. Talent wasn't. Vanity didn't have much talent. In two months she called home for a ticket back. Back to safety and some kind of throne. In Los Angeles they didn't even know she was gone, cause they hardly knew she was there.

Her daddy smiled sadly, gladly sent the money, borrowed money. He had been sending her so much to keep her in the style she thought she had to have, to keep her happy, he was most broke. But he was happy he was gonna have his "baby" back! Her Guardian Angel must have smiled with relief cause a whole lotta things wait for pretty girls in them big busy cities.

She returned to her little three-legged throne. Told everybody she didn't like it in L.A. because the people had no class. But she read that writin on the back of that throne, looked at the horizon again, saw "marriage."

Now . . . one man, Robert, really worshipped Vanity. You know right there he was a lightweight fool. He had done gone to college and had a future, but the future wasn't there yet, so he was still in the strugglin stage. He sure knew how to talk tho. And he could kiss her from the feet up . . . she had to have that! He wrote her poems. Sent her flowers. Kissed her feet. Used his eyes as mirrors for her. Since she saw herself so much in his eyes, and thought he had a future, she married him. Her daddy surely did go into BIG debt for that weddin. I blive he still owe some on it and he dead and gone now!

The mother and Mega came. The mother lookin sad, Mega smiling with joy for her sister. She wasn't asked to be in the weddin. She was married now, with one child. Vanity said she needed a pretty matron of honor with some money so she could get a better present from her. She seemed to understand Vanity, didn't seem to mind, but I knew she was hurt cause she was a family person. She cared. She knew how to love people for real reasons.

Anyway, the Guardian Angel must have held its breath, but the marriage lasted only three years. Til Vanity was twenty-five. Turned out Robert's struggle was lastin too long . . . and the kisses didn't last long enough, cause they got borin and all tied up with cookin (in gloves) and eatin, going to the bathroom and snorin, his dirty clothes, underwear and all, and blowin noses and payin bills (she made). He be tired and she need another dose of worship. She took to leavin him snorin and going out to get what worship she needed, in them expensive clothes she charged on him. Her daddy was still payin for some of her clothes too, she sure could spend money on herself. He was still livin then, poor fool. She never did buy nobody else nothin!

Now, Vanity didn't go too far out. Not very much adultry, cause that wasn't what she was after. Just more love and worship. A few times she did commit adultry was cause her worship bank was low and she couldn't get that worship no other way. She ended up have two abortions for two reasons. One, she didn't quite know whose baby it was. Two, she was never gonna mess her body up with nothin! Her husband never knew. Her daddy never knew. Even her hairdresser never knew. Just her and the one who gave her the pills and things, and me, cause I had to help her, care for her.

Now that took a little toll on her looks, but it didn't show right then at the time. That little bit of drinkin, she loved champagne, didn't do much harm, but it did some. She liked to smoke cause it made her look classy, she thought. That took a toll, too. But you couldn't see it cause she made-up and dressed-up so good. But . . . she still got bored after awhile. Her Guardian Angel used to whisper things to her conscience to make her life fuller, more satisfying to all. But it found nothin there to listen to it.

She got divorced. She didn't get no job tho. She lived off the money from her father and what she could get out of her ex-husband. She could work with that money. Somebody else's! Cause she wouldn't work FOR it.

Then she made friends with a wealthy older woman, Snity. Snity spelled her name "$nity." Her new friend was almost just like her, so $nity didn't let Vanity round her husband too much. $nity did go all the way with her admirers. She was growin old and losin her beauty from livin so hard and much. She did introduce her to other wealthy men tho.

Vanity was a good catcher for $nity and was used as such for a long time, til she was thirty or thirty-one. She got to travel, go places she never could have gone before. She was lonely, so she was sleepin around a bit. But you had to give her some money then, cause she needed clothes to keep up with $nity. Her Guardian Angel weeped.

Finally a older man came along who $nity didn't want. Name Edward. The man had some little sense cause he had made a lotta money. But, between $nity talkin him into it and Vanity bein so beautiful (still), he asked Vanity to be his wife. Vanity opened her arms wide, showin all her beauty at once, and flew to his side like a Condor jet! Guardian Angel held its breath again.

As life would have it, Edward got bored early with the kissin from the feet up. Wanted hisself kissed from the feet up. But mostly he wanted someone to share his mind with. He took a clear, longer look inside his beautiful wife and . . . HE got bored!

The man still had some sense, so he took the good from the marriage. Vanity was a good hostess, handled his business meetings at home well. Could socialize successfully. He kept her. And she kept him. In time, tho, she became bored, less men paid attention to her. She became lonely. Edward wasn't often interested in makin love and worship to her. He became lonely. No one to really talk to in his home. She didn't care for his grown children. They were uncomfortable, so they just gradually stayed away. He had to visit them. He was welcome, but it wasn't like bein at his own home. Guardian Angel shook its head in sorrow.

Edward liked Mega, even did some business with her husband who was moving right along with his business, using elbow grease and brains. But even Mega didn't come

round much cause she had three children that Vanity didn't
like.

No, Vanity didn't seem to like children at all. Edward
didn't know it, but Vanity had already had one abortion with
him. It was his child and he sure would have loved it. The
child would have tied them closer, into a family. Guardian
Angel wept again.

Another thing Edward didn't know, Vanity was workin
with a doctor to plan a appendix operation which was really
goin to be a historectory. She told me she could not keep up
them abortions. She had got real sick from the last time and
thought Edward might find out why, for real, if it happened
again.

She looked over at me, over that glass of champagne she
had brought over to my house and said, "I simply cannot
afford to ruin my body. Not for any baby, nor any man! My
body is all I have, and I am not sharing it! The baby will end
up with all my looks and all I will have is a 'baby.' "

The woman was a lonely woman, very lonely inside all
her beauty and didn't know how much a baby, her own
child, could mean. But the baby might have been lucky not
to have been born, after all. I don't know, cause I don't
know everything. So, historectory it was.

When Vanity got to be round thirty-five she was runnin
round like she was crazy. Going to every party, every show,
every night club, about every night. Driven dissipation. She
was desperately trying to be rich and happy. Sometimes her
despondence and dissipation was pitiful. She cried. But not
too long, cause it made you ugly. Her tears musta been
champagne cause she drank it all the time. Carried a bottle
in her car. Opened. Guardian Angel asked to be relieved of

its duty. Devil grinned cause he likes destruction and confusion.

She kept that up til she was round thirty-eight years old. Beauty goin cause beauty ain't somethin you can beat to death every night. Edward was so bored, disgusted, tired of everything so empty, he was in pain. When I say, "bored," don't take that word lightly. "Bored" can be miserable, miserable. That is what he was, miserable. And each month the bills were higher. He was payin plenty to be miserable. Divorce came on his mind, naturally, cause he never was a real stone-fool.

Mega's husband died round that time, too. She was broken nearly to pieces by his death. She truly loved him. Theirs was a good marriage. She had the children tho, and he left her pretty well fixed. Edward, of course, went to console her. In her innocence, he was consoled. She looked healthy and warm, too. And her house had lots of love in it.

Vanity's and Mega's father died round bout then. Death comes like that sometime. In threes, people say. His heart was probly broken, cause it sure was starved. Vanity didn't never have no time for him in her fast life. He was like some child she didn't want to be bothered with. She was in New York partyin at the time. Called and told Mega to decide everything and take care everything, see bout the insurance money. That she would TRY to get back in time for the funeral. Guardian Angel tried to quit.

I was her friend, but I got mad at her then, and didn't know whether I'd keep on bein her friend or not! I could see how she might do me one day! Or anybody! Her father did everything she ever wanted! She never paid no time to her mother either, but that old woman made it so she didn't need

Vanity. She had her Mega and grandchildren. I know she would have loved to be closer to her daughter Vanity tho. You know mothers.

She did make it to the funeral . . . late. Mega did all the work need to be done. Mega cried the most. The mother too. Vanity cried, with a glass of champagne in her hands all through the funeral, what was left when she got there. Edward was disgusted . . . again. He had his arms round Mega, consoling her, more than he had em round Vanity.

Well, now . . . Vanity had all the money she needed, but them admirers was fadin away. Edward was fadin away. Vanity was lonely, unhappy. Her beauty was really fadin away too. She decided to go in for all that plastic surgery stuff. Edward put his foot down, then he put his marriage down. They got a divorce. Now, she really was alone. Lotsa friends don't last long sometime. Vanity was very, very lonely with only herself. But that was the main person she had loved.

Everything happened so fast. Edward and Vanity divorced and we looked up and Edward was marryin Mega, who probably saw in him the father she never had. He was good to the children too! Neither one was marryin for money cause they both had some. He older, but they still together and it look like they happy to me. That whole family! His kids is welcome now to his home.

Vanity like to died, sure nuff! when they got married. She said Mega had always tried to take everything from her she ever wanted. Lied. She consoled herself by tryin to take every dime she could from him. She told everybody her sister had broken up her happy home. Lied. Friends (?)

smiled and turned away. Guardian Angel had a sore neck from shaking it.

Vanity was thirty-nine years old then. She spent plenty money on that face surgery. It did some good. Then her mother died. She said she couldn't let herself cry like she felt, cause her operation was too new, it would ruin it. But even with them operations, she was beginnin to look like her mother. She had mirrors all over her house. She would see herself all day, wherever she moved. Sometimes she just scream, break out in tears and run jump in the middle of her sumptuous bed and cry, tryin to hold her face straight.

Vanity went into retreat. Wouldn't come out for nothin. Ordered everything brought in. Chile, the woman was somethin! Layin out there in that big ole house with all the rich stuff in it. Lonely and unhappy . . . and scared. She had never lived like that before, and she didn't know what to do. Everybody who would help her was gone . . . or dead. She was alone. No mama, no daddy, no close sister, no child. Alone, chile.

Mega who was nowhere near her in looks had her husband. Vanity knew something was wrong. The men were gone. She was free, divorced, and the men weren't rushing in. It must be her beauty. She really stayed out of the sun. Spent hundreds of dollars on lotions and creams, magic formulas. Like a lady, she thought. Her Guardian Angel looked over the world, saw the starving, the sick, and cried. That was the saddest angel!

So . . . she lived her life alone. Retreated from all her "friends" and "admirers" for, to her, the reason for their admiration was fadin away. She wanted to be remembered as the most beautiful. The most beautiful lady ever in their world. Yea . . . so she retreated from the world. Like a lady. Her Guardian Angel took a deep breath, sighed and rested in defeat, but hope.

But . . . no matter what you do or how you hide, this world, life, is not going to let you get away without livin. Long as you breathin, something is going to happen to you!

Her life proceeded in a quiet way. All her days was spent alone. She might talk on the phone just to keep up with what was goin on in her old world. She didn't want any company. Maybe $nity, but $nity didn't want to come nowhere dark and quiet. She was old, but she thought she was still goin strong, tho now, she was givin the men her money.

Vanity told $nity, "You are a fool! Givin somebody all that money you have worked hard lyin, layin and marrying for! A man wouldn't know how to fix his lips to ask me for any of my money! I'll never get that old and need any loving from anybody who expects something for it other than my time and my beautiful body!" She laughed. "I don't need anybody, or anything that bad! A man coming into my life better bring something with him!"

After long days, bathing, drinkin, creaming her body, wearin her lovely delicate negligies, drinkin, eating, lookin at TV, staring out in space through the curtains of her huge windows, drinkin, listenin to records, starin into mirrors, drinkin again, she was bored and restless, but did not want to go out where people were. She actually thought she was gettin ugly, but she really wasn't ugly. Older, naturally, but, she didn't look bad as she seem to think.

She lay in bed at night, lonely, longing. Staring at the mirror over her bed. Wishing for someone. Her first husband . . . no. Her second husband . . . maybe. Rainy nights were the hardest. She played blues records and, yes, some-times she cried. She felt sorry for herself that everyone had left behind, somehow. They say the blues ain't nothin but a woman cryin for her man. Well, she just didn't exactly know who her man was. He had to be in her past. Sure didn't look like he was in her future.

Sometimes . . . she felt just like the dogs she could hear howling at night. Oh! Lord! They sure must have the blues, to sound so, so sad. So blue. Even lost, deserted. So lonely . . . in the darkness of the night . . . in the rain . . . in the quiet. Sometime she would cut off all sound, music and TV, in the house and lay and listen to the sound of dogs callin to each other. Mating calls. Sad longing songs that sounded full of need and painful feelings. Alone. In need. Alone.

Her life was so quiet, she began to look forward to orderin things somebody had to bring. The groceries was the most likely thing, cause she did like to eat good food. The liquor store, too, was the most regular delivery.

The man who delivered the liquor was very mannerable, respectful, quiet, youngish . . . bout thirty-eight or thirty-nine years old. Always smiling. Gentle, smooth, smart. Knew how to do a million things around the house that always need doing and always did a few before he left. Hang a plant different, move a table, a large chair. Fix a small pipe, see why a light didn't work. All those kinds of things. You know. All the things some women wish a man was around the house for.

He never touched her. Even accidently. No, no. He re-mained mannerable, never familiar, never out of line. Didn't even curse a little bit. Just never did anything wrong. You know. Like I say, the kind some women wish was around the house. He was good-lookin too. Bright, youngish face. Hell, he wasn't old anyway.

He liked good music. It got to where she always searched for something new to play for him . . . to hold him a little longer. Then it got to where she had something fixed for him, something he had said he liked to eat. He drank very little. She ordered so much liquor to get him over there, she could have stocked a speakeasy. She liked to see him. He was just about perfect. Her Guardian Angel became alarmed. Because, you see, the angel knew.

Yes, he was almost perfect. He had practiced a long time. He had several older women he always delivered to. A few with money, they had to have money, had even become what they thought was "his woman." He made love to them. Good love. He was gentle sometimes, rough sometimes, but always only just enough. He never did anything too much. With them.

He had a nice life. Just deliver liquor. His customers bought so much, the owner let him handle just the ones he wanted to deliver to. He could do something extra if he wanted to. He had wanted to deliver to Vanity. He had watched her for several years. She hadn't seen him. Until she was alone.

He wouldn't live with any woman. Wanted to be alone, free. Wanted everything he wanted and all he could get of it. He really didn't want for nothin, not with them ladies he had. He dressed, always in good taste, very expensively. He liked hats and he sure looked good in em!

He knew when not to see someone. He was a bit cruel. He could ignore either one of his "women" for a week or two. Send someone else with the order. Not call for two or three days. You know. They always end up givin him what he wanted. He never asked, just mentioned. And he only mentioned once. So you better remember what he said and hurry up and get it if you wanted him comin back.

Vanity came to expect him. To count on him. Even to love him . . . a little, and he had never touched her. Yet. Her Guardian Angel whispered to her, but she really couldn't hear the angel I guess.

His name was Jody. Jody was born, I think, with something left out of his soul. The ability to love somebody, anybody, but himself.

Yea, he came into her life. Yes, chile. Ain't it the way life is? Just keep foolin round with it . . . it will fool back with you!

Jody had all the charm, all the manners, all the look-like concern and care for the female race they needed. He was warm and affectionate with his voice. Color of a sunny Hershey bar, lookin just as rich and sweet. Warm, admiring eyes and a gentleman to the hundredth degree. Six feet tall, large shoulders, played football and basketball in school and college. Yes, he went to college and still just a delivery boy. He wore bikini underwear. Don't ask me how I know! He, also, had five children he claimed were all not his.

In two months, they were close, old friends. Watchin the results of all they had done in the garden at night. Vanity would only come out at night. He smiled that warm, sweet smile and started workin with her. He had to build some new shelves on his day off, for all the liquor she had bought. He never asked for a dime. Never accepted a dime. Anyway, that started him spendin most his days off with her. One of em anyway, she didn't know he had all of em off if he wanted to.

Then, his television broke. He could fix everything, but he couldn't fix his own stuff. Naturally they spent several evenings, just friends, lookin at TV. Somehow Vanity mentioned, in a laughin voice of confidence between friends, how she loved to make love in the mornings, and when it rained, when it stormed, when it thundered. You know?

One day, when the weather report said "rain, storm," he came by that night, to check on her, of course. She sat down and lay back, in one of them flimsy rich gowns and looked at him. He was quiet, but he knew how to look back. He looked so good, so big, so strong. Vanity squirmed, crossed her legs back and forth, all them things we do. She finally jumped up when the programs was finished, news, weather and all. Jumped up and said, "Go! Please go! I . . . I . . . I don't know what's wrong with me! Please go."

He smiled a warm intimate smile, said, "Talk to me. Tell me what the matter is."

She couldn't.

He said, "Am I your friend? I guess I'm not. And I . . . I feel so much for you. I want you to like me. But . . . I know you can't." He looked down into his drink, then back at her, deeply. "You are so beautiful. So beautiful. You could talk to, or have anyone you want in the world." He stood, as if to go. Vanity raised from her seat, but she didn't stand, just sat up. He went on talkin, "I am only me. So . . . I understand. I'm not . . . something enough for you."

Vanity slowly got to her feet, reached one hand out to him. "Oh!" Her other hand touched her throat. "Oh, you are everything wonderful to me. You are my friend. The only one I have. Do I really look beautiful to you?"

Jody reached out to her slowly, with that warm hand. Took her arm that had brushed against him so regularly lately, pulled her to his side. She buried her face in his shoulder. He used his chin to nudge her head around til their lips met . . . then he kissed the shit out of that woman.

Moments later, with heavy breathin from both of them, he said, "I better go . . . I'm only a man . . . and you are a beautiful woman. I won't be able to control myself." And he left, even tho she was holdin him and pullin on that man for all she was worth. He left. And she longed.

Vanity went to the phone, ordered more liquor. A big order. Then she went to her dressin table, made up her face. Perfumed her body. Soon the deliver came, Jody brought it. Not long after, she came. Jody brought it.

His time had come. The next time she saw him he said, "I am ashamed to have taken such a liberty with such a beautiful woman of whom I am not worthy." You ever seen or listened to a woman convince a man he is worthy of her? Well, all I can say is her Guardian Angel wept for her.

Vanity told him he was worthy of her when she came again . . . and he went away, satisfied. She came . . . he went . . . and that ain't the same thing. You know it! But Vanity fell asleep, satisfied. Like a lady?

When she woke up the next day, everything else did too. Passion, love, need. All for a man whose address and telephone number she didn't even know. A man she didn't even know what his dreams was. A smiling man she didn't know, who brought her liquor when she ordered and paid for it. A stranger. Maybe we are all strangers, but, Lord, help a woman at such a time in life where she will put her heart in strange hands full of blood and tears. Lord, help the men, too, cause it's all kinds of strangers out here.

Jody didn't come back with the next order . . . nor the next. A young, young boy did. Vanity like to died. All her morning had been about getting ready for him. She called the store and asked for him . . . he was not there. She had no-where else to call and the store owner could not give her his number, he didn't know it. Finally, in a few days, he just dropped in about 11:00 at night. Her heart bloomed, opened, screamed out at the sight of him. He had come again! And so did she. But this time there was fear in the coming and she did not sleep so soundly satisfied when he left at 1:00 in the morning. The heart that had blossomed, had wilted with a little hurt pain. He gave her no number, no address. Said he had no phone and was never hardly home anyway. Always lookin for a job to do. He had huge bills to pay. "But, no, don't worry, I will make it." He said, "I don't want your money." She had offered, of course. She loved him and his painful beauty.

The next week passed. No call. No visit. When, finally, he did come, all the anger she had planned, vanished. She loved him who loved her beauty. For the first time, he had brought her something . . . a lovely golden mirror. "A magic mirror" he said. "So you can see your beauty framed by me." Vanity looked into that mirror all the time. All the time. Like a fairy princess . . . preparing for her prince.

In the following months they kinda had a relationship, least a year and a half. He still came to her at his will. She was always ready because he took so long. Sometime, when he and his regular girl were on the outs, yea, you know he had one, he would stay a day or two. Til he and his regular girl were together again. The regular girl woulda missed him for the two days and be eager to mend things. He would have lain around, eaten, watched TV, made love once, slept . . . and thought. He would then have to go see about his other regular old ladies, also.

Sometimes he would come to Vanity and sleep only on top of the covers, while she lay beneath them, body smoldering, longing for him to enter her. But he would not get into bed . . . let lone into her, tho she begged.

Jody did not kiss her from the feet up. For the first time she longed to kiss him from the feet up, but was afraid her beauty would not look good from that distance. He kissed her lips . . . when she asked him, or when she seemed to be gettin tired of longing for him, ready to quit her grief. He would not see her for five, six, seven, eight days at a time. Let her suffer.

He made dates with her. Then she would do a lot of cleaning. Herself! Cooking, setting the table, puttin out flowers, all of it. Then, looking out the window, sittin, waitin for him. . . . He did not come. Then . . . she looking into that magic mirror . . . to see what was wrong. She saw lines, wrinkles that were not there. In that mirror, when he did not come, and she could not . . . her beauty faded, faded.

She began to buy him clothes, lay them all out on the bed. If he didn't come . . . she would want to throw them all away, give them away. But, she never did, because she had the good sense to know she really wanted this man and would need something to lure him. She "forced" money on him, which he never asked for, just needed, but he took. He folded away, smiling, hundreds of dollars that disappeared deep into his pockets, never to be seen again.

Valentine's Day. No card. He didn't call.

Birthday. No card first year. Only a card the next year . . . late.

Christmas. The second time. A handkerchief. Not wrapped.

Easter. No card. No eggs. Not even his.

Thanksgiving. Said he had to work, needed the money. She cried, again, for she had cooked a full, good meal . . . for him. She couldn't eat.

All the time, he was having a good time with the money from his other little old ladies and his woman. Yet . . . he really was with nobody in his heart. Nobody at all. Vanity spent so much money on him to ease the worry he said was on his mind, made me sick! I mean, really sick, I got ill.

Vanity asked that man to marry her. Marry her! She wanted a lifetime of all that pain. That's what she was askin for! He said he had never planned to marry. He didn't trust women to be true to him. Now! She tried to convince him of her love and faithfulness. He thought about that, a long, long time. Sometimes, he looked into that golden mirror he had given Vanity. Looking at his own beauty. Thinking of marryin Vanity. Of livin in the dark, cause Vanity kept her house darkened. She thought she looked better that way.

Once or twice, when he had come to Vanity, he had been a little sick. She cared for him better than anyone else he knew. Vanity! Caring for somebody else! In a day or so, he always felt better and left with some money.

When she spoke to him of marriage again, he thought a

moment, then asked for the use of the little roomette she had in her yard in the back. She gladly gave it to him, tho she said he could stay in the house with her til he decided. Til HE decided. Her Guardian Angel just stayed quiet and grieved all the time now.

He took the roomette, but did not LIVE in it. He used it a lot. He liked to be alone, he said, so she often just looked out at the little house, glad he was out there, close. She would cook and take him food. Sometimes he didn't let her in, said he would be on in her house, later.

Often, when he did come in later, he would be so shinin and sweet to her. He kissed a lot and spoke much of her beauty. But he didn't make love much. He sure talk to her tho!

"My lord! You are so beautiful! So beautiful to me! How do I deserve you? You could have anyone in the world you want you are so beautiful."

Vanity's answer, always, was, "But I only want you."

She began to pester him about lettin her come visit him in the little house. "What did he do there? Couldn't she be with him? She would be quiet, not bother him. He wouldn't have to make love to her. She wouldn't ask him or touch him." Can you magin a woman sayin that to her man?

She told him one day, "I always look so beautiful to you when you come out of your hideaway. If I was in there with you, and I was quiet, I could look beautiful to you longer. In there."

He said no, and no, and no, no, so many times. Til he looked at her one night, thoughtfully. She was sittin there with little tears in her still lovely eyes, waiting, waiting for any little sign he loved her. I hate to think she was such a fool!, but I don't know bout this kinda love!

He answered, touching her cheek, "Soon."

"Soon" came one night when he needed some money and asked for it for the first time. She hesitated, cause she thought that would help him leave. He read her mind, said, "I will let you come with me to my hideaway." She gave him the money. He left. He was back soon this time.

He looked at her another long time. Then sighed, and said, "Give me one half hour, then come."

She did. Her Guardian Angel cried aloud, screamed to her, "Beware!" then wept again.

The little hideaway was darkened. Persian type blankets and carpets covered everything. A small, low table on the floor was draped, covered with little saucers and things. He sat her down beside it, smiled down at her, warily. He then picked up a pipe. A pipe he used for free-basing cocaine.

The Guardian Angel could not come in, but he pounded at the door and screamed for Vanity to hear. She did not hear. She was looking at the man she loved, smiling. Just like a lady.

Jody fixed the pipe. Used a lighter to heat the stem til he reached the rock inside and melted it. Drew the first breath, blew it out. Took another breath, closed his eyes and held it in. Opened his eyes, smiled, and handed the pipe to her. Said, "Do what I do."

His hand reached out, slowly. His beautiful, powerful, strong hand that had held her, stroked her, seemed to love her. He held that hand out to her with the cocaine-rock, crack, in the pipe. She already loved that hand. She remembered only the pleasure it had held for her. Her eyes, lovely tho wrinkled around, misted, than clung to his smiling face.

She took the hand, that then gently removed itself from the pipe, leaving it in her once lovelier hand, then gently raising it to her once lovelier lips. Her eyes held to his own. Just like a lady.

Then? Then . . . she slowly finished lifting the pipe to her lips, closed her eyes with the imprint of his smiling face in them, pursed her lips and drew her first breath from the pipe. The magic pipe. She opened her eyes, the smoke wafting slowly through her body, inundating her brain, while looking at this gorgeous man. Then she smiled, raised her beautiful head, parted her lips . . . and blew . . . her . . . life . . . and all her beauty . . . away. Forever.

Just like a fool.

The devil slapped his knee, leaned back and laughed.

The Guardian Angel gave up. On its knees, beside the garden house door, it wept. The angel's voice was silenced by the golden pipe, the golden man. The golden pipe had a new voice to whisper in her ears. The Guardian Angel could only come back if she sought it. It will wait, even for nothing.

So . . . I'm just sittin here, lookin into this magic golden mirror Vanity has gave me because she could not bear to look into it anymore. She could not see the self she sought. The golden pipe has lied.

PLUS, I know she needed the money I pressed into her thin little hands. Almost all her beautiful things are gone . . . sold for that wisp of smoke. And that man she can never have for her own.

I am ponderin . . . ahhh, ponderin . . . thinkin about life . . . and death. Love.

Ahhhh, but so much happened. So much I didn't know about til way much later. My heart aches for her, but . . . it was HER choice, HER life.

In tryin to understand what had happened to my friend's mind, her life, I searched, asked questions of them people who knew her then, were her friends. Friends? I will tell you what I found out. It was pitiful. And if you got youngsters, you better listen to this first, then decide do you want them to hear this truth. This is just one day in the later life of Vanity, just fore she died from a heart attack, a broken, busted-heart attack.

Early one wintry morning after bein out all night til bout 5:00 A.M. . . . Vanity went inside the shell of her large, once beautiful house, empty now. Everything being sold, piece by piece. First, by Jody, then, at last, when her need was great and she started doin crack without Jody, she sold her own things, her own self. So the house was empty now.

The house note hadn't been paid in thirteen months and was soon to be foreclosed on. Gone. All her usta-be dreams. Gone.

The lectric company had turned off the lights. The gas company had done turned off the gas . . . and it was cold, cold, cold in that house. The water was the only thing on cause Jody knew how to turn it back on after the water company turned it off. So Vanity could drink water out a paper cup or a leftover tin can. Didn't need no water for cookin cause wasn't nothin to cook. She didn't have no appetite anyway for nothin but more crack . . . them bumps, them hits of rock. She was thin, thin, thin. Skin and bones. Somehow, she managed to keep her phone workin, cause she had to be able to get them calls from them fellows who might give her a bump. A Bump!

This particular night, and I know now there were lots of these kinda nights, she had been workin for that crack. She didn't call it "workin," but I do.

Jody was no longer the only man in her life. Now, she had had all kinds of men. All kinds. Kinds she wouldn't even use to spit on! Them "Bumps" had sucked and bumped all her pride out of her brain. That shit must be some powerful, cause you remember how full of pride she was!

Now . . . from the lowest person in a garbage can, man or woman, to the crack dealer who was the highest she could get, even they only wanted to use her for a half-hour or hour. Not even them so much anymore cause they had all already tore her down, stripped whatever little dignity she mighta had left. Yes, the bottom was as high as Vanity could go now. Them old days was gone. Like her beauty. Like her health. Like her life. Gone. No future to it. Nothin meant nothin to her now but that next bump, that next rock. Low-life crack users called her a "Rock Star," laughin and graspin their crotches. I heard about em!

See, she had a big reputation, well deserved, they say. She was known, far and wide, as the best "head" in the city . . . and anything else you wanted you could get from her if she needed that crack! Her! Can you magin?! Her?

Anyway, she had come into that empty house that dark wintry morning. She closed the door, leanin back against it. Tired. Worn. She looked at the phone tho. It wasn't ringin. Then she felt her hunger. She hadn't eaten in bout five days.

She didn't have no energy. Her mouth tasted like sex from goin down on eight men in the last ten hours. Two others had refused her head, preferred anal sex. So, besides her mouth feeling used, stretched and bad, her rectum was bleedin a little.

Little pains shot through it now and again, cause of the huge . . . organ . . . one man had smashed into her, hard. She had cried out, but he laughed and stuck his chest out in front of the other men (yes, chile, they do it in front of everybody!) and thrust harder. She wanted to scream and tell him to stop!, BUT she wanted that rock he had promised her. That crack. If this is what it cost, well, she didn't have no money, so . . . this is what it cost!

When he, finally, finished and it was time to give her her reward, her bump, he decided to tease her . . . and degrade her even more. He melted the crack on a pipe, took him a big deep puff of it, blew the smoke at her to make her want it more. He was smart, he knew what he was doin. He leaned toward her, offering the pipe with the crack to her then, pullin back when she reached for it. She loooooooonnngggeeed for that pipe.

Involuntary, she snarled and lunged to snatch the pipe. He saw her comin . . . He caught her in the top of her long, used-to-be-pretty, hair and pulled her face down to his penis what was still coated from that anal sex they had just finished.

He told her, "Lick it clean."

That stopped her a moment, brought her back to some ooold reality, the times before she ever thought about crack. When she was beautiful and only dealt with the best of people. She felt disgust. She started to say "No!" and shake his hand from her head. BUT . . . then . . . her eyes fell upon that pipe in his hand. As he knew they would. She remembered that big rock he had just melted in that pipe. All thoughts of disgust just flew away. She closed her eyes . . . leaned over into the man's lap . . . and cleaned him with her tongue . . . her mouth that sits right in her face.

When he had had another orgasm, this time in her mouth making her swallow it, he let go her hair he had been pullin. She raised her head, lookin down at the large, limp penis . . . for the rough spots that felt like sores to her tongue. They were there. She wiped the back of her hand across her mouth and almost gagged. But didn't. She wouldn't allow herself to think about the sores now. She needed that pipe now.

She sat up, didn't even pull her clothes straight fore she asked, "Give me my hit now?"

He, that piece of cancer sore, looked down at her with contempt, looked at the other fellows with laughter. He sank back comfortably, flicked his bic and heated his pipe stem, moving the fire to the end where the cocaine-rock was, then he took a pull, a hit. He thought it was a real good one, so he kicked back and let the death hidden inside the good feeling reach into his body and brain, chippin away at what was left of his sanity. He did not know that in six months he would be dyin from just what he was doin now . . . and from them sores. He would be slave to the King Crack then. He was already, just didn't blive it, but he would do anything for it too!

But, now, he just laughed, and thought how he had got over on her. Humped her from the behind and then stuck it in her mouth to clean it! All them users had the same aim, like he did. They was so low they just wanted to degrade, humiliate other people, specially women. Then, too, it was because she was so beautiful once, it still showed. He had never ever even talked to anyone who had been so pretty and almost rich. He knew she would never have even looked his way, if she had not become this . . . thing . . . called a rock star. They would do the same thing to a ugly woman, but they wouldn't enjoy it so much, or gone so far . . . maybe.

He looked down into Vanity's pleading eyes, waved the pipe in front of her face and said, "Bitch, I ain't givin you nothin! The best thing you can do is get your funky, dirty ass out of here!"

She cried out, "You promised me!" Wiped her mouth again with the back of her hand, "Give me my bump!?"

He looked at the other fellows, laughed, said, "You just got your bumpin! Get the fuck out of my face, ho!" (That's short for whore.)

Another fellow there felt a little sorry for her. He didn't really like to see people dogged, til it was his turn. He wanted to speak up, but he owed the crack dealer some money and he wanted some more crack hisself, so he didn't want to mess up his own game. So he sat back and let it all happen. He laughed a little too. He thought to himself, since he felt sorry for her and knew she was walkin, that he would give her a ride home. Then she could clean herself up. Maybe . . . even give him a little head fore he went home. He didn't want nothin else from her cause he knew how many men she had to go through to get some crack and he didn't want no disease to take home to his wife and kids. He musta not known you can catch a disease from a mouth too!

Vanity never did get her bump, her hit. They put her out instead. The man hurried and begged up on his rock then rushed out to catch up with Vanity fore she found somewhere else to go beggin for crack and he lost her. He wanted that head! He drove and caught up with her, offerin her a ride home. Fore he got her to her house he told her they would look for some crack. He got his head. But he pulled to the curb front of her house and put her out, sayin, "Let's try later, baby. I'll try to get hold of some money. You try to get hold of some too. I'll call you." Then . . . he drove off with his crack deep down in his pocket. His own wife didn't know he was a user. Or that he already had that bug in his blood that would kill both of them . . . just from makin love. That's all his wife did to get it, make love to him, her husband. Chile, chile.

Anyway . . . Vanity was home. Home? Her back against her door. Hungry, wet, cold, dirty, stinkin and sick. She never had got that bump. They had just used her, again.

Her body wanted to sleep, but she couldn't get that bump, that feeling she wanted, out of her mind. Her brain raced, trying to think of somewhere, someone, she could get some money from. Sell some head to. She thought briefly of Mega, but Mega had loaned her so much in the beginning, never gettin it back. Now Mega watched her so carefully when Vanity was in her house because she had lost so many small valuable things that Vanity could put in her brassiere or under her dress. Couldn't go there. The early mornin time never entered her mind cause when she wanted some dope, she didn't care bout no inconvenience to nobody else.

Sellin some of her head came back into her mind. Vanity's mind snapped back to the man who had had anal sex with her then made her clean him with her mouth. She remembered the sores on his penis. She worried: AIDS? Syphilis? Gonorrhea? Herpes? What? She pulled her tired back away from the door, went to wash her mouth out with the peroxide Jody kept there for when she made oral sex to him. After she did other people in front of him sometimes to get both of them a bump, he didn't like her to do him without washing her mouth out. Jody never wanted her body anymore. That is, when she did get to see him. She couldn't see him noway less she had some crack to share.

She rinsed her mouth. She didn't think of the fact she had swallowed everything and that peroxide couldn't reach it. Then she lay her tired, abused body across the old, dirty quilt thrown on her bedroom floor. She fell asleep . . . for awhile.

The phone rang! She jumped awake to answer it. It was a fellow saying he had a rock he would share with her . . . for a little fun. She told him to come on over.

He said, "No, we . . . I rather ride awhile."

She quickly answered, "Okey, I'll be outside waitin."

They came. There was two of them, fellows. One got out to let her get in the middle and they drove off, sayin they was goin to somebody's house. They had the rock.

She asked, "How we all gonna use one rock?"

They laughed, answered, "Ahhh, we share all things all the time."

But they drove too long, too far. She became afraid. The feelin in the car was not good. The men were groping over her legs, her breast. She kept pushin their hands away.

She asked, "Where we goin? Where is the rock?"

They laughed and turned off the highway. Who needs to tell it all?

They finally stopped. Pale, early mornin. Deserted woods. They made her get out, go down, lay down, then go down again. She cried all through everything. Mad cause they had fooled her and there was no rock. Then they talked awhile to decide should they take her home or not.

One, the "nice" one, said, "It's kinda dark, man, and cold. Let's take her back into town anyway." So they did that. But they never did give her a bump or puff from their pipe. Why should they? They had had all the fun they wanted anyway. Well, at least they didn't beat her too. Yes, they did that to her sometimes.

Vanity still ain't had no food.

She didn't have enough clothes on, she was frozen almost.

She ain't had no real sleep for almost four, five days.

Her body is stinkin and dirty, again.

But her brain still wouldn't think of nothin but that dope. That bump. That puff from a pipe. What kind of stuff must that be that can strip you, make you do ANYTHING to get it? Take everything away from you? House, furniture, automobile, bank account, clothes; yours and everybody else's you can get your hands on!? Takes your honor, your dignity, your pride in yourself. Your very life! I wouldn't even want to SEE it, much less use it! It scares me to death!

Well, she came to my house. She looked so bad, so sad, my heart broke for her. She wanted to "borrow" some of my little, hard-earned money. She already owed me plenty fore I got wise that she wasn't gonna buy food or nothin she needed. Just dope.

I fed her. Ran bath water, gave her some clean clothes. All mine was better than all hers now, and I really didn't have nothin special. She lay down and slept. I took advantage of that to wash her clothes and run to the store to get somethin better for her to eat and to cash a small check to give her a few dollars of my small money.

When I came back . . . she was gone. So was my watch I was stupid enough to leave layin on my dresser. My only watch what had belonged to my mother. I loved that watch! I cried. I know that crack took my watch, not her, but it was gone right on.

Vanity didn't stop to pawn my watch, I mighta got it back if she did. She took it straight to the crack dealer and got her three rocks for my beautiful watch. Then she went home and blew my watch away . . . in a hour and a half. Just like that!

At last, her body just dragged her down to sleep. And even while sleep she waited for that phone to ring. When it did ring, she went out again . . . and everything started all over again.

All over again. All her whole life now, given up for a bump, a hit, a puff, a feeling. A little piece of death . . . that had such a hold on her mind that only a full death is stronger. Or God. But she wasn't likely to run into Him. Her Guardian Angel wasn't allowed to go into the places she went into. Her Guardian Angel just sat over her and wept sometimes when she was home waitin for a call. It did that til she died, then they parted forever, and it went to its home, sadly sayin, "I hope I never have to go to Earth again."

Five years is all it took. Five years of days just like the

one I'm tellin you about. She lived all that, every day, over and over and over again. And, surely, some worse ones I don't know about.

I couldn't do it, couldn't take it. I don't want nothin that strong to kill my life and me! Do you? Would you?

So . . . I am sittin here ponderin . . . ahhh, ponderin . . . thinkin about life . . . and death.

Love.

And Vanity.

Lord, Lord.

I
TOLD
HIM!

I'm kinda mad about a lot of things, but I'm gettin better. For instance, bout my life. It's my life! And I found out sometimes you got to fight other people bout lettin you live your life your way! I know you gonna think I'm crazy. But I ain't! I just haven't never lived too long doin things my way with myself. At first, I didn't know what I wanted to do bout everything, but I sure did know what I didn't want to do. But people don't care bout that! People just care bout what THEY want for you to do! I didn't never plan my life the way it went. But, I bet you right now, I'm sure gonna be the one decides from now on just who I'm gonna let drive me crazy!

Just listen to me. Pleasssse! I'm gonna tell you bout it!

Now . . . when I was in school, a little, little girl, Wallace always got some way to get to be round me. Wallace was the worsest, baddest, meanest boy you ever want to meet in your life! He was a ugly little boy . . . and mean! He sat behind me in every class I ever had in school. Always pullin my braids, jerkin my head back, oh! all kind of things did Wallace do to me. When he couldn't touch me, he just stared at me. I told him not to do it, but he did it anyway! I just hated to see him comin at me every mornin.

All the while we was growin up, he did so many things to make my life miserable, I just don't know how to tell you. All through school he jerked, kicked, pulled, pushed, tried to kiss me! He took my sweaters, tore up my notebooks, stole my homework, ate my lunches. Just stare at me when the teacher catch him. Oh, I told him not to do it, but he did it anyway! We grew up that way. At least, I grew up, he just stayed the same stupid dunce!

We had to grow up, alright, nothin can't stop that but death.

At recess, or lunchtime, he use to make me sit in one spot. Better not move, or he would hit me! Always threatenin me! Ball his fist up and make me cringe. Stare me down. Wouldn't do it to nobody else. I use to pray to God to please let Wallace like on somebody else. I didn't care bout givin no bad luck to nobody else, I had done already had enough bad luck of my own called Wallace! No matter how I tell him not to do somethin, he'd do it anyway!

By time we got ready to graduate junior high school, I just knew things was gonna change. That Wallace would go on and be in some other classes. Leave me alone cause there be so many other kids there for him to torture. Well, that didn't work out cause Wallace took most every class I took, whether he liked em or not. I told him, begged him, not to do it, but he did it anyway!

All cept the auto-mechanic class. He REALLY didn't like that class. I kinda liked workin with mechanical things. But I really took it cause it was the only thing he wouldn't take. I guess he thought the other fellows would see how dumb he was, compared to them. He said he knew he was gonna be a butcher like his father, so it didn't make him no never-mind bout what he took in school!

That's the way I HAD to grow up, cause nothin coulda stopped Wallace but death.

All through high school he kept doin bossy, controllin things to me. And things was gettin to be pretty important in my life. Things I needed to decide for myself, he was decidin for me! He had done told all the other boys not to mess with me, I was his! They was scared of him cause he was so bad and didn't fight fair. So, you know they didn't mess with me. NONE! I told him not to do that, but he did it anyway!

Now, along come prom time. Everybody graduatin and all, excited and lookin forward to the prom to wear your first grown-up formal dress. That sposed to be the best time of your school life. I really wanted to go. Dreamed on it! And I sure don't have to tell you, I did not want to go with Wallace!

Chile, nobody would ask me on account of Wallace! He's the only one asked me. No . . . he told me I was goin with him. Stared me down.

Now, every time Wallace force hisself over to my house, he be the most different boy you ever want to see, in front of my mama. He have the most manners, be so polite and clean and helpful and neat. In front of my mama. So you know, naturally, she really liked "that Wallace boy." I tried to tell her not to, but she did it anyway.

I studied hard in school, got good grades. I was goin on to college. Had my grants and everything. That prom was important to me. Mama knew how bad I wanted to go, what it meant to me. So when it came to the prom and nobody else ask me, Wallace told my mama he wanted to take me. Now, you know she couldn't understand why I didn't want to go if I had to go with Wallace. She talked and talked to me. Finally she got mad, said, "You goin to that prom with Wallace. Ain't nothin wrong with that boy! You just a ole hard-nose girl! What's wrong with you?! You better get dressed and take your behind outta here to that prom!" I tried to tell her not to do that, but she did it anyway.

Well, goin to the prom would have been alright except for after the prom. Wallace had a car. I got in, kinda laughin and happy cause I had had a almost good time even with Wallace there. Maybe cause I just knew that that was gonna be the last time I was ever gonna have to be round Wallace all the rest of the days of my life. But, after we got in the car, Wallace took me way out on the highway into the wild part of the country and MADE me, forced me, to let him make sex with me!

Besides havin my best new dress on that me and Mama had done worked and saved for, I never had done that before and didn't want to. I fought harrrrd. Tore my dress. Tore my stockings. Messed up my hair, pullin it. It hurt. It hurt. I hated it, I hated him. I told him, begged him not to do it . . . but . . . he did it anyway. Anyway!

I sneaked into the house when he finally took me home.

I shouldn't have done it. I should have let my mama see what her Wallace choice had done to me. But I didn't want her to see her daughter who had left home so pretty comin back in the condition I was in. I knew it would start up a whole lot of stuff. So, I decided, since I never had to set my eyes on Wallace again in life, nor get in his car neither, I would just let it pass. I shouldn't have done that.

Now, I ain't quite learned bout who makes all the big rules in life, but life sure can be mean and hard sometime. It didn't have to happen, but it did. Two months later, when my life was goin on pretty fine, I realized I was pregnant! I tried to hide it, til I could decide what to do, or if there was anything I could do. But, in some way, my mama could tell what was happenin to me in my body.

She asked me, "Who did it? Who did this to you?!"

I told her, "Your favorite! Wallace did it!" I was scared to say he raped me. I didn't want big trouble. I sure didn't want her to think I let him! So I just answered her question.

Then she said, "Well, that little man will just have to marry you!"

I liked to died! I pleaded, I begged. "Please don't make me marry him! Don't do it, Mama! Please. Let me have my baby on my own. I'll take care of it. I'll work. We don't need him."

But she insisted. "I'm callin him over here right now! He gonna do the right thing by you. He is goin to marry you!" She called him.

I begged her not to do it, but she did it anyway.

He came over, not even shamed. Just lookin proud and mannish. They the ones who talked. Nobody ask me nothin! And it was my baby and my life!

You know what he said, "If she hadn't ask me to do it to her, I wouldn'ta. But you know I like your daughter. So . . . I did." He stared at me like I better not correct him!

My mama asked him, "Well, do you love her at all?"

He told my mama, "Yes, I love her and I'll marry her!"

I begged him, begged him, not to do it, but he did it anyway.

With my mama behind him, believing him, we got married. I cried all through the ceremony down at the city hall. They thought I was cryin cause I was happy. Some people did look at me kinda funny tho, cause I know my face didn't look like no happiness! With me holding on to the doors tryin to keep from goin through? I know I didn't look happy! But people tends to believe what is SUPPOSED to be is. I whispered to everybody would listen, "Don't let em do this to me." But they did it anyway.

Oh! I hated it. I hated him! I didn't love him at all! I didn't want him to touch me on my weddin night. The most precious moments in a woman's life. I spent mine cryin while he had his honeymoon on me.

Bout seven months later my little beautiful brown baby was born. Oh! I loved it! It was mine. Not his. Mine.

Life became a regular thing for me. By regular, I mean he regularly beat me cause I didn't enjoy his lovemakin. I mean he regularly had other women, by the dozens. They called the house and came by when they got ready. Didn't think nothin of me. I told him not to let them do that, but they did it anyway.

Why did he marry me? And who in the world would WANT to call him? Why didn't he marry them?

He drank, regularly. Got traffic tickets, accidents, all

that. I told him not to drink like that, but he did it anyway. He spent his money on other women, gambled, everything! I told him not to do it, he did it anyway. He fought me, abused me, gave me nothing of value for ten years. Ten years of pain, fear, tension, sadness, and finally boredom, even with fear and disgust. Cause I hated him on top of me. He just stare down at me while he tryin to make sex. I'd tell him not to do it, but he did it anyway.

I came to slavery and hate. Yes, I slaved. And I hated. He wanted all things in all the wrong times. Midnight, he wanted supper, specially if I was sleeping. 4:00 A.M., he wanted breakfast, specially if I was sleeping and I usually was. Isn't everybody? All day, every day, any hour, he wanted sex and he was using other women too! I was scared to say yes because I didn't know if he had just got some disease from somebody, I was scared to say no cause I was tired of bein beat! I'd tell him not to do it, but he did it anyway. Every time.

I had gonorrhea eight times, siftless three times. I PRAYED he didn't bring nothin home they couldn't cure. Oh, I told him not to do it, but he did it anyway.

Now . . . I am not a mean woman. I am not a jealous woman, at least, not of him. I haven't ever had a chance to see if I would love and be jealous of anyone else, he has run my life so much. I am not an envious woman. But I HATED. I hated him. I told him what he was doin to me, but he did it anyway. Just stare me down, laugh and walk on away.

Round bout that time, whenever it was, I started gettin jobs. Because we was always short of money all the time, naturally, cause he had to pay for his fun. My husband worked good, when he didn't have a hangover or was layin round tryin to sue somebody from some accident that was his fault! I tried to save some little of whatever I made. Cause I had a child, and I had a dream! I had that dream ever since the first minute I got married. But everytime I got some money together, he would find it! Then spend it! On liquor and women. I told him not to do it, but he did it anyway.

I just felt lost. Lost! Well, what can I say? What do you feel when everything keeps gettin lost? Your dreams, your money, your life? . . . and seems unreal? My life was so unreal. I KNEW people was livin better than I was. I knew people was in love with the person they married. I knew families was happy together . . . sometimes! Not me. Not mine.

I had two kids now. He just took it, raped me when he wanted to. I told him not to do it, but he did it anyway. And we still wasn't a family.

Now, life didn't leave me all out in the wilderness by myself. God is good. I had made a friend, down the street here, at the gasoline station. The man who owned it, Mr. Evers, a little older-type man, but very kind, very nice. So different from that man I was married to. Mr. Evers helped me get a little ole car on credit from his gas station. He knew Wallace tore up every car we got and I had to get to the baby-sitters and things so I could work. That's the kind of person he was. He knew I needed help and so he gave it. I liked him.

When I got my car, such as it was, I told Wallace not to drive it. I needed it and I never knew when he'd be home. He just stared at me like I was crazy. And sometimes when he came home he had had a accident and our car would be unable to drive. Of course, you know, Wallace drove my car when he felt like it. When he came home, it usually have a new dent in it. If he didn't hit something while he was gone, he hit my tree I planted side the driveway long time ago. My tree I named Baby. I loved my tree too. He was killin it! I hated that cause I took care of my things. I'd tell him not to do it, but he did it anyway.

I didn't have any friends. He didn't like nobody I liked. Said they wasn't no good, would lead me wrong. Lord! Him and my mama had done that! But my mama wasn't so crazy bout him as she used to be. He was still nice and mannerable in front of her, but she could see them black eyes when I had em, and that time I had the broken arm. She knew. But she didn't ever say anything to me about it, because she knew I had told her not to make me do this, but she did it anyway.

My life was just in shambles. All I had I could truly say I enjoyed was my children, cause I counted them mine. I was just miserable allll the time. I cried for what looked like to everybody else no reason. Just out the clear blue sky.

I thought about killin myself, taking my own life! After I thought about it awhile I knew I didn't want to leave my children. And I told myself, "You ain't got no business wantin to kill your own self! Your self ain't the one makin your ass unhappy! He is! Don't kill yourself!" So I didn't.

Meanwhile, I was doin a little extra work for Mr. Evers, the garage mechanic man with the fillin station. Typin, filin, billin, cleanin up the place, things like that. He paid me well cause he knew I needed the money real bad.

Then, that time came when Wallace wrecked my car real bad, Mr. Evers got it down to his shop for me. I was cryin. He hugged me, for the first time, and told me not to worry, just pattin my shoulder. Then I felt his hand slide down my back a little too far. But I didn't have no money and didn't want to worry bout my car, so I didn't say a word bout that hand. Just stood there cryin and leanin on Mr. Evers.

He said, "You know I always liked you, Ella Lee."

"Did you, Mr. Evers?" Sniff, sniff.

He smiled and patted. "Yes."

I sniffled. "I'm sure glad somebody do."

He rubbed. "I'll fix your car for you."

I sniffled loud and wailed, "But, I ain't go no money, Mr. Evers."

He rubbed harder. "Wellll, we'll work somethin out."

I looked up at him, sniffled softer. "What we goin to work out, Mr. Evers?"

He looked down at me, still rubbin. "Well, we'll see. Do you like me, Ella Lee? A little?"

"Oh! Mr. Evers, sure I like you. You bout the only friend I got." I didn't count my mama too much since she was the one made me marry that Wallace. She didn't have no money for my car either.

He bent his head down to me, "But . . . I mean, do you like me a pretty good piece?"

I kinda laughed. "I like you a whole lot!" I did, too! He was always kind to me. Concerned for me. I sure did like him! I needed that.

His hand slid all the way down my back and patted. I liked it cause it was gentle. He didn't GRAB me and GOUGE, PULL me round like Wallace did!

Somebody drove in and he moved away, said, "Well then, we'll work it out."

And we must did, cause my car got fixed.

Now, Wallace was very jealous and mean-minded, so the only way Mr. Evers and me could make this thing work out was for me to work longer hours for him in exchange for him fixin the car and later on he would give me extra money on the side. It worked. I'm so glad. I needed kindness.

I really started likin my job. I always liked mechanical work anyway. Grease and all. Don't know why, just do. I was learnin how to do a whole lot of things on a car as well as the book-work too.

I, also, got to likin Mr. Evers too. He was real nice. When we would slip off together to "get along," he was so different from Wallace. He was gentle . . . and kind. He would massage me, all them pains Wallace gave me. He would bring along a little gin with orange juice, put them old Billie Holiday records on, and then make love to the music, real slow . . . and gentle. First, I thought it was cause he was older. Now, I know it's cause he just know what he's doin. Yes, sir! I grew to like him a lot. He was the first man I had picked for myself. The second man in the whole world to make love to me. And he really cared . . . for me. If I told him not to do something, he didn't do it!

I still was havin a horrible life at home with Wallace. He had just lately found my new hidin place for my money I saved for my children. He took it, spent it on just nothin! His women! I told him not to do it, but he did it anyway. He beat me pretty bad bout hidin that money too. Throwin me all up side the wall and all. Two black eyes, arm twisted so bad it untwisted like a telephone cord almost! I begged him not to do it, but he did it anyway.

Mr. Evers was really mad, but what could he do? Wallace would kill ME sure-nuff! He wouldn't do nothin to Mr.

Evers! He ain't gonna hit nothin but a woman. Not going to hit no man.

Now . . . I love my ass. And I was pretty damned tired of havin it beat!

When I was a little better . . . almost, Mr. Evers said out the clear blue sky, "Let me show you how to fix your car so nobody will be able to steal it without bein hurt." I watched and learned how to fix them wires round and do a couple things extra I knew already on my own. I already had one dream. Now I added a plan.

Now, please don't think I am a mean, ugly person. I am not. I was just tired of bein so abused, not listened to. Lord, have mercy on me, I sure didn't mean to do nothin to nobody. To hurt nobody!

But, I did fix my car with the wires and everything, right on the side of my house where I lived with Wallace, in my driveway. And I did, when he came in half-drunk from somewhere off with his women, tell him I had to go off . . . and "NOT TO USE MY CAR CAUSE I WAS GOING TO USE IT WHEN I GOT BACK."

I started down the street, went back to the house and said again, "Wallace, DON'T USE MY CAR. I MEAN THAT." Then I went on bout my business.

Least I thought I could. I really had not gone far when my mind told me, no matter what anybody did, I didn't have no business gettin mean as they were. I turned round and started runnin back home. I was goin to tell him what might happen if he use that car before it got fixed. But I was too late! I saw him steppin into the car. He saw me comin. He laughed that ole ugly laugh of his. Stepped on the starter before he closed the door.

I screamed, "DON'T DO IT, WALLACE, DON'T START THAT CAR!" But he thought I was still tellin him what to do, and . . . he did it anyway.

Now . . . I don't know how all this happened. It was just gonna be a little ole small explosion. But good thing Wallace hadn't closed that door. The car blew up! Wallace was blown sideways out the car door, then he went straight up! Don't ask me how all that happened, where all that power came from. I guess that car didn't like him neither! He went straight up in the air, don't know how many feet, and he came down in my tree, Baby! Baby like to beat him to death as he was fallin down through the branches. I told Baby, "Get him, Baby, get him!" Baby got him! When he hit the ground he had whelps all over his whole body I could see, from them tree branches whippin his behind! And you know how he use to always STARE at me, like he was tryin to scare me or something? Well, he don't stare at nobody no more, cause when he finally came down and hit his head on that cement in the driveway, one eye looks up and the other looks down! They don't look in the same direction no more! But . . . he can still see. One thing at a time.

Well . . . I told him not to do it. But he did it anyway.

It didn't kill him. I didn't plan to. I wasn't goin to mess my car up so bad I couldn't find it and fix it!! I wasn't plannin on goin to no prison neither for no man on this God's earth! But, he did have to go to the hospital for some broken bones and things. And bout his eyes, but seems they couldn't do nothin right away. Said one day they may just straighten themselves out. He was gone four, five weeks and after that he came out on crutches.

So . . . I had time to save for my dream. My dream . . . since the day I was married, was my divorce. And I got one!

I moved out Wallace house. I didn't want nothin from there. Not even the house either. Wasn't nothin there noway, but pain and sufferin. Mr. Evers rented me and my children another one for a little while, til he could buy us one. Ooohhh, yes! I liked Mr. Evers a whole lot now!

I don't know what I would have done without him. He helped to give me knowledge and helped me with money. A person needs their marriage partner to be a friend sometimes. See, a older man that's still good is hard to find. And a good man that's older with some sense is hard to find, cause they usually all taken. Catch you a young one, good and with some sense, you done got you ten gold stars from heaven! That goes for good women too! Sometimes they hard to find too!

Now, it's my fillin station. We work there, Mr. Evers and Mrs. Evers, side by side. My children are happier, cause it's peaceful in our home. And sides that, it'll be their station one day. They can even plan on college now. They got a brand-new little brother now, too. I named him "Fore" cause his last name is "Evers."

The only thing is . . . the other day my son from Wallace was going to do something and I told him not to do it. But he did it anyway! Now, I know I wasn't able to stop his daddy from goin under my dress to get him, but I also know I ain't havin another Wallace comin out from my own dress for me to raise and live with! I whipped that boy so hard, Mr. Evers had to stop me.

Mr. Evers said, "Quit whippin that boy, Ella Lee. That ain't Wallace you whippin!"

I told Mr. Evers right back, "He MY son and I know what I am doin!" See, I blive if a whippin is right, if they can feeeel it, you may not have to whip that child again for the same thing. And that might mean his life! Who gonna want him if he like Wallace? Not me! And I'm his mama. So he got whipped.

This morning, when I told him not to do something . . . Well . . . he let "something" alone.

And Wallace. Well, his one dream now is a drink and a place to lay his head at night. Even his butcher daddy is sick of him. He stay drunk all the time now. He is killin hisself. Just killin hisself!

Everytime I accidently see him . . . I always tell him, "Don't do that to yourself Wallace. Don't drink yourself to death." Yes, I tell him not to do it . . . BUT. . . .

NO
LIE

Everybody talkin bout how Time is such a great, forever, long thing, makes me wonder why the little piece of life we get is such a short one. I know I could use a couple hundred years more, cause the time you do get, ain't nothing but enough to show you what you oughta have done with the time you done already had. Then, you be done got to the end of your life and ain't had time enough to really, really use what you done learned. No Lie!

Like in the beginnin, when I was born? I was a beautiful bouncing baby boy! Then I was a pretty youngster growing up and a good-lookin handsome man when I was grown finally to be a man. I know what I'm sayin. No Lie!

My mama say the first thing I looked at in this world was the female nurse. I knew at that minute I loved women. Been lovin em ever since. No Lie!

I learned about sex at a late age, bout eleven or twelve years old. I took to it right away! When I got to be bout nineteen or twenty years old I was Jamming everything would stand still long enough.

I had done learned the cardinal rules from them old men, and some fathers, who tell all the young boys how to grow up to get to be smart young men. They tell you all kind of things. I can't remember all of em, but some things was, "You don't need nothin fat but a bankroll." Or "You don't need nothin black but a cadillac!" Even "You don't never fool with nothin old but gold!" And "Don't never fool with no yellow woman, they evil. They sleep with their fists balled up!" And "Ain't nothin right about white women but their money!" Or "If they brown, keep em down!" All such a stuff like that forms many a boy's education when it comes to women. We learn it from the old men almost while we takin milk from our mama's breast. My brother, he's older than me, he laughed at them old men, but me, I listened to em! And learned!

Now, this woman tellin you my story don't like me to talk like this, but when I looked at my private piece one day, I named him "Beau Jam." Beau Jam! Well, that's cause that's what I was doin, you see. Jammin everything I could. All I thought of, morning, noon and night, was women. That stuff filled my head. No Lie! If I could'a made love to myself, I would'a! I'd kiss it if I could! I loved my body cause I loved makin love with it!

Remember from school, that story bout the stepmother?

And that mirror, mirror on the wall? Well, all my early life I looked for one of them beautiful mirrors for me to look in. I finally found one and had to pay bout $400 for it! It was worth it! It was so beautiful it made me more handsome. I have carried that mirror with me everywhere I been. Still got it! Yea, I loved my looks!

The women loved me, too! Well, liked me, I guess, cause I never stayed long enough for none of that love stuff. No. No. I had to keep movin on to some place new. There's too many women in the world to stay too long with just one of em! No Lie!

Sides, I like the romance part at the beginnin. That's the best part. The beginning. I like that eye business, when you first meet somebody, or you spot em cross the way. You can tell, too, sometimes by just lookin at the lonesome in her face, the need in her eyes, just how soon she gonna say yes and how long it will take to be in her bed! No Lie! You can even tell by the way she's built, just where everything is gonna be! Now, that's the truth.

Yea, I like that eye business. Then comes the "talkin that talk" that's kinda fly and witty and sweet. Excites your nerves some, upsets you in the right way. Sometimes, tho, they can turn you off right at the start! Didn't too many turn me off tho, cause I knew I wasn't gonna stay too long no how. So what I care how dumb she was, or how anything she was? My brother was always lookin for a "good" girl. He sure was a fool. What you gonna do with a good girl?

Anyway, when you like em, it's the best, more fun. No lie! But you already know that.

Then . . . them little accidental touches start. Them

brushes of the bodies. Yeasssss. You can tell how a woman gonna be in her lovemakin like that sometimes.

Then, you finally gets to the kisses. The first one is always sweet . . . always sweet. Cause, see, she think you is her future husband. While I would be counting the time, she be seein a husband, maybe. After the kisses start, it ain't gonna be long then fore you get what I came for. See, I believe in the hereafter . . . and I know what I am here after! I get it too! These ladies have changed for the better. I like this liberation stuff! These new liberated ladies will do most anything to get what they want!

Sometime, after the lovemaking, I be happy awhile, cause she be happy, you see. She be playin house. Shopping for food, cooking them nice meals, buying some nice little things for me. Like house slippers to be used round the house. Make me feel at home so I can think I want to live with her in holy matrimony. Yes . . . everything be nice, real nice. Warm and cozy. You can get all you want! My brother wasn't gettin hardly any, the kind of woman he looked for! Sometimes you could get money too. But I didn't always look for that.

Then . . . things always begin to change. Cause they just got to ask that one bad question. "Do you love me?" That comes bout the second night you stay with her. Well, hell! You got to say yes! I did! Cause maybe I wasn't through. Then they keep askin it, and it's something some women feel and know cause some of em didn't blive me. They want me to get married and prove it! So I knew it was time to go . . . and that's what I did.

I members some of em start demanding things. Like proof of my love. Wellll, that change things right there. Soon

. . . I start being a little late when I meet em, go visit. Then a lot late, cause they don't raise up off that love stuff. Why can't a woman be satisfied with a little lovin from a good man?

Then, she want to know who else is in my life. My life! Hell, do she really think I'm going to tell her? No, Lord. Not and mess up all my good things for Beau Jam!

So then I start not showing up at all. Cause it ain't no fun no more. They done messed it up! She done took all the laughter and joy out of the thing. She got to pout and fuss before you can make love. That make the love-makin sad. So, soon, I ain't goin there no more at all. Just drop it, cause I ain't got time to beg and fuss bout no lovin. It's another one out there who ain't pouting and fussin. They ain't hard to get cause they lookin for love . . . and they don't always can tell what it look like, so I get in a whole lotta doors with a imitation key. Ohhhh, Man! That was fun! No Lie! Well, It sure felt like fun. My brother, that fool, didn't have but one girl then.

Now . . . you leavin the woman alone cause you don't want to fuss, then she don't want to leave you alone. Calls you, say, "Come by my place," stuff like that. You know what they want when they say, "Pleeeeeasssssssss?" But by that time I be done sized up some other woman and I be gone on a new thing. Then I look up one day and the same thing done happened with the new thing . . . and I got to move on again.

Wellll, a lotta time in my life passed like that. Just going long havin fun. Hell, I was young. Didn't think too much about time. I looked up one day, seemed like only a year had passed, but it was ten of em and I was thirty years old. Had a few babies behind me and a whole lotta pretty women. Ain't gonna tell you bout them ugly ones, but they sure-nuff got somethin what makes them look beautiful sometime. No Lie!

My brother had done married his woman. Wasn't he nothin?! I laughed at him. Wastin all his health and good lovin on one woman! Havin babies. He was tryin to go to college at that time too! He wasn't havin no fun!

Well, I didn't marry bout them babies. I told them women not to have em cause I wasn't no marryin man and had a lot to do in my life fore I could be a daddy to anybody. They went on and did it anyway! So it ain't my fault. I told em that was their business, not mine. So . . . I still didn't get married. Some called me "irresponsible," but I don't care! I was too smart for that! What I really was, was irresistible! Noooo lie.

Noooo . . . I finally left town. Moved to a bigger city. More pick and choosing. . . . Lord, I've known some pretty women in my days. And, quiet as it's kept, I've known some good ones too! I . . . think of them sometime. Sometime . . . I think of them kids, too. They don't even know their own daddy. Somebody told me one day, maybe them kids was lucky. I know they was just havin fun teasin with me tho. I like to think it's sad them kids will never know me.

Anyway, I don't like to talk about that . . . cause it's too sad.

Anyway, I went through that new town just like the last one. Had me a BALL!! Had a good job, a nice apartment. Furnished it off to a living T and I LIVED! You hear me? I lived! I had a wardrobe would burn your eyes up! Yes, I did! No Lie! Man, a woman couldn't turn me down if she tried.

But they never did try. Not too many of em anyway. I was somethin!

Those women I met in those years when I was between thirty and forty years old had more money and liked to do things for me. Was good to me. But it got to the place I couldn't tell the new ones where I lived cause shit just kept poppin up.

I got shot once. Yea, some fool woman shot me. Me! And all I was doing was makin her feel good! Some women is a fool!

I got cut two, three times. I can show you! No Lie! It's some women you better look out for, cause they don't play! They spend that money or cook that food or clean your house and wash your clothes enough and you better be where they want you to be when they want you to be there. And that's no Lie!

Anyway, I looked up one other day and I had two, three more kids by two, three different women, had had to move from the place I lived bout five or six times. Got put out by the landlord once for some woman was disturbing the peace. It was her fault. Cause I never disturb nothing cept sheets. She didn't have no business comin by my place without callin noway! I already had the company I wanted for that night! I don't like to fuss and fight. Later on she say she just had the blues. What's that song say the blues ain't nothin but a woman cryin for her man? What she spect to have when she got me? I understood her, but she still shoulda called!

Guess I just got something these women can't live without. Gets good to em! Man, they won't let go! No Lie! Ole Beau Jam.

Sometimes tho. . . . I remember one night. I went out one night and I looked up and seen one of the prettiest women you ever want to see in life! No Lie! And . . . that pretty woman didn't give me no hard time, no long time, to catch her either! Man, Beau Jam was in seventh heaven.

But I didn't spect no problems cause I was dressed to the last inch. I member I had on some pale, pale yellow gaberdine pants, clean and sharp. Had a pair of Stacy Adams shoes such a light tan color they just seem to match them pants perfect. Had on a pale green silk shirt with my ascot. Yea, I wore them! Seen em in a magazine and liked em, so I got some. I had money. Anyway my ascot was patterned gold and dark green, and my jacket was a forest green, rough wool fabric. I was sharp! No Lie! Man, I was clean! No Lie!

She said we couldn't go to her place, so . . . against my new law I had for myself, cause this woman was too fine to let get away over some silly law, I took her to my place. Picked up a fifth of scotch on the way, good scotch too. Rushed in, changed my bed for this pretty woman while she got the ice and the glasses, threw a little cologne on the hair on my chest, put on my loungin jacket, silk, and strolled on in to the feast. Ohhhhh, lord.

Wellll, turned out it wasn't such a hot piece of feast after all. I really could have done without it, easy. Sorry I didn't. She left later that night takin some of my best cologne with her, stole it. I don't know where she went or how she got there cause I didn't give a damn. It was that kind of lovin, you see. Then, bout two, three days later, when I had to go to the doctor cause you can always tell when you got a problem . . . I found out I had a case of syphilis! I sure did want to know where to find her! No lie! Cause she messed up my life!! I mighta not never been able to make no more babies! And I'm a man! I need to be able to make babies! Sides that, I had done made love to two other ladies of mine I knew. And now, all hell was gonna break loose if I told them! No Lie! I could'a whipped that woman's ass! Yea, I do that sometime too! You have to teach a woman somethin sometime! I sure will whip one! My brother, he always talkin to his wife. That make women think you weak!

Anyway, I called both of my ladies up and cussed em out for what they had give me!! It worked on one, so we know what kinda lady she was! She wasn't no lady! She was a tramp! She musta been makin it with somebody else. The tramp! She wasn't no good! The other one cried. She had never had a veneral desease. But she was a fool if she thought I was ever gonna own up to that one.

Anyway, it was time to get ready to leave town again. Gave up a good job too! By the time I got to the new city I was going to live in, it was my birthday. It felt like only a month before that I was thirty years old, in my prime of life. You hear me! Lookin good, feelin good, lovin good, everything good. And here I was forty. Forty! Jesus!

Now, even tho my brother was older'n me, he already had a paunch belly, he still looked good. Always laughin. He had a different job now, a new profession since he got out of college. They had done bought a house, was raisin kids. Still, that fool ain't never had but two or three women in his LIFE! I bet he fools around on the QT tho, even if his wife does still look good. I checked her out! She looks good! She too serious for me tho! I didn't see them much noway, cause he always tryin to tell me how to live my life!

Anyway, after I moved I got another job, soon, cause I

had only a little savings from all that partyin and my car. But I got a apartment. I was in that apartment getting ready to meet the lady down the hall in the building I lived in, and I was shaving. I looked hard in that beautiful magic mirror of mine and my face looked different to me all of a sudden.

Round my eyes was little puffs. They use to go away in the mornings after I wash my face and such. But this was evenin and they was still there! No lie! I leaned in closer and do you know what I saw in my face? on my chin? Gray whiskers! Only a few, but there they was! No Lie! Jesus. I checked my hair on my head and, true to life, there was them gray hairs right near my ears. Only a few, but Jesus! There they was.

I took my tweezers and plucked and pulled them damn things out. I went on out that evening. But the next day the gray whiskers was back, and the next week the gray hair was back! Back again! I found out wasn't no sense in pluckin and pullin cause I would be bald soon enough already. I could see that cause my forehead was gettin bigger, goin further back. Hell, I was only in my prime of life! No lie! Or is it? Wasn't no fun lookin in my magic mirror no more.

Well, what you gonna do? I met a few more ladies. Glad, cause the one down the hall is too close and I done quit foolin with the ladies on my job less I just can't help it, cause that usually runs into trouble. Sides, women ain't hard to meet, no color.

Round that time, tho, for some reason I don't know, and I don't tell eveybody this, I went with a man. I know, I know, I know what you gonna think. But . . . I don't know . . . he was one of the sweetest, tenderest persons I ever knew. It felt a little strange, cause I am a man! But . . .

when I held him in my arms, after, I didn't feel like I was holdin no man. I felt like I was holdin a person, a tender person with needs, with love in his heart. A scared, tender, little person, with weaknesses just like everybody else. Desires too. Could he help it what he wanted?

I mighta coulda stayed with him longer, but he wasn't happy and I knew I would never be happy cause something just didn't feel right about it. So I just stopped going back. He was better than most women cause he never said a word.

Now . . . these ladies in a big city seem to demand more, least they did of me. Young girls wanted some money for some pretty little thing or something, even the rent sometimes. So I didn't fool with them too much no more. I took on the older ones who they say appreciate so much. Well, they out there, but they got demands too, and they didn't always want me! You hear me? I was gettin turned down! No Lie!

Plus, even tho I didn't make but one baby during that time, this time she was going to take me to court! Shit! I hurried up and got on way from there. Went on and moved back to my first town where I grew up. Went to my brother's house, he had a bigger, better house now. Two of his kids in college, the girl, pretty, was married. They had grandchildren! Fools growin old fore their time!

Thought I'd look around for my own kids, they was older now, hell, they was almost grown. But them I found was callin some other man "Daddy" and they mama didn't want to even talk to me on the phone less I had some money to give em for what they said they had gone through without me. Well, that was that! So much for me tryin to be a father to my kids. I hope they learn someday that they mama stopped them from knowin their own daddy.

Now! It seem like it was only a week since when I was forty, but I looked up and I was fifty. Fifty! Fifty! I didn't even bother to pluck and pull nothin! I rather not no more. Hell, I was about bald on top and the sides was full of gray hair and my whiskers too. I kept shaved. Gave up my mustache. That damn thing was gone gray. Even round Beau Jam was gettin gray.

The time I should have been in college, I wasn't. I was busy makin love. So I had to start takin them lesser jobs. Paid less. Didn't look or sound too fancy either. Usually had to wear a old gray uniform made my skin look gray. So nobody knew me where I worked. I just worked the job and left it. Quietly. Went on home.

Home. Wellll, with less money, I had to take a smaller, less expensive place, so I just went on and took a room. I didn't spect much company. Wasn't nobody visiting me noway. No lie! I just put my magic mirror on them dingy walls and sat down. Didn't even look in it. It still was beautiful, but I wasn't.

Five years zoomed by. Beau Jam let me down a few times, even as good as I had been to him. No Lie! So I began to call him Beau Jelly . . . yea.

I was fifty-five. Wasn't makin love too much at all. Maybe five, six times a month. What I use to do in a week! No lie! Met ladies now just to have some way to get a home-cooked meal. Sit in a warm comfortable house or apartment and listen to some good music sides this ole buzzin radio. Smell some little piece of perfume when the lady passes by.

Some don't even play good music. And some of em, all I

hear is false teeth rattlin as they chew or grin and check me out, wonderin if I'm going to let them down, which I often do now, just can't help Beau Jelly.

But least they got somethin of their own. Most got kids or grandkids comin over to visit them, or inviting them over for all the holidays and rememberin their birthdays and Mother's Day. Ain't they got a Father's Day now? I really try to get them holiday invitations cause that's when you get to really eat all that good food and be round a family. You know, kinda warm. Yea . . . kinda warm.

Lately I been sittin and countin up the years til I can retire. Six years or so now. Don't know what kinda money I'll have comin in, been on so many jobs, so many places. There will be somethin, I know that, cause I been a workin man. I never did try to do no pimpin or livin off no woman. The harm I did was the harm they liked. Wasn't no harm noway. I know that's no lie.

Not too long ago I met me a lady at the senior citizen place where they have a dance once a month. She bout sixty years old, I guess. Got some money left her when her husband died. Got a nice house, nice car. Mine just rattle all over, the one I had to get cause my pay is so small.

You know what I did? I fixed my mouth to propose to her, ask her to marry me. Me! No Lie! I knew she needed a man around and would be glad to get one like me cause I still got some of my looks and I still dress nice even if I only got two suits.

You know what . . . ? That woman just smiled and preened and laughed . . . sound like happy laughter, so I laughed too. Ha! Ha! Happy laughter. But when she opened her mouth, she said, "No . . . I'm sorry. I'm just not ready." You hear that!? She said no! She don't know who was proposin to her! Me!! Who ain't never proposed to nobody! I gave her that compliment!! And she say no. Well . . . times change. Times sure do change. No lie.

Mostly now, I go home, fix some supper, beans or somethin out a can, in my little kitchenette. Wish for some cornbread or some dessert. Drink a can of beer, most times warm, cause this tiny ole half-butt refrigerator don't half time work. Then sometime fall asleep lookin at my second-hand TV. Sure wish I had saved some of that money I used to party with! I have spent thousands of dollars to have a ball and to feed Beau Jelly. All my life . . . was spent lookin for one piece of a woman . . . and they all got one just for bein born.

Sometime I wake up and it's dark and cold in my room. For awhile I don't move, can't, got arthritis a little. And I think of my life, my kids . . . and try to think of someone I could call my woman, my own . . . and I can't. Just noways can't.

I am so lonely . . . so lonely sometiiiiiime, I could DIE! No lie.

I sure wish that I had met some lady I could'a loved. . . . Maybe I did and just didn't even know it. But women ought to be . . . should oughta . . . they oughta . . . If they was better people I know I would'a stayed with one of em. But they must not be no good. No good for nothin but lovin, cause you can't trust em. They don't mean no man no good. They don't mean right.

Just like them babies of mine, they grown now. They mamas should have told them I was the daddy! Then today I'd be a grandfather. I'd get stuff on Father's Day . . . and

THE
DORAS

You can look up from anywhere you are and the
world will look HUGE to you in your mind. Sky look big and
wide . . . just going everywhere. Now, everybody, everywhere, all over the world can do that. And everybody everywhere can almost, ALMOST, make they life close to what
they want it to be. It's true! A great big, busy world, that's
all they is to it! And look at what all you can do in it!

When we start out we all gets life in this huge world on
the first bein born head-out! Can't go back and say, "No, I
don't want this, give me that, please." Just got to go make do
with what you got give to you when you born.

Look like some people get so much more than others.

Even get some money, which this huge world loves. But
. . . I have seen sometime, in this world we live in, that
most things balance out, equalize out, in the end. Yes, in the
end. Cause some people take nothing and make a whole
heap out of it. Just like some people take everything, another whole heap, and let it run down to nothing. Human,
chile, human.

Now this here town where I am is a small place now, so
you know what it was then, near the beginnin of this century. Had some shopkeepers, a little ole bank, a lawyer or
two, cause they always makes a livin, people being what they
are. Had a couple doctors, a few teachers, a little city hall, a
pool hall and several bars. A market for food, or two. And
little mama-papa stores. It was small, chile. Everybody tryin
to make a livin.

Some people do what they done learned in school.

Some people doin what they mama and papa taught em.

Some people doin whatever they can with whatever they
got.

Some people sell they blood to make a livin.

Some people multiply they blood, just livin.

Speakin of multiplyin, let's speak of Dora.

Dora was born to a mother who had seen the tail end of
slavery, any kind you want to think of, but not the end of
hard times. Dora would'a come from a middle size family,
don't know was she gonna be the youngest or near to it. I do
know many a day the mama licked her fingers and drew em
cross the bread box and the crumbs she got there was her
supper.

The mama didn't have nothin but a no-count man. Her

own mama was dead, sister's poor, brother's gone. She just didn't have nothin.

One day they was gettin ready to move again to go find work on somebody's cheatin farm. She looked at her childrens and her eye fell on Dora, who was another man's child, not her man's, but was hers right on. Even then, at five years old, Dora looked strong and thoughtful . . . and hungry. Mama said to Dora, "Go . . . go and get fed. Ain't nothin for you here, ain't nothin for nobody here. Go." She didn't quite tell that child the truth, cause love was there and that child's mama was there.

Anyway . . . where she sent Dora, the child didn't get fed much there either. Some . . . not much. She was sent to be a orphan. Her piece'a family left town with her mama lookin back, sad and disgusted, weary heart wailin the blues. I don't think Dora's mama smiled in the rest of her life fore she died of TB. Dora didn't do much smilin either!

Dora was there bout ten, eleven years. I don't know. Couldn't count. She was there tho, and they, that orphan home, was poor too! Didn't nobody worry bout givin them nothin cause everybody who cared didn't have nothin to give. Them rich people musta been too busy cause . . . well, let me tell you.

Them orphan kids was fed, but they was fed so little, and the food wasn't much nurishin, bein that they had to take what they could get and stretch that . . . like beggers do. That made them kids mostly sickly, and you know there wasn't much of no doctor to see to em. If there was one, you had to watch and see just what he was bad at, cause them good doctors was mostly off makin money with richer folks.

All them children had they own little cot and raggedy

blanket, sometimes clean, sometimes not. Well, I'm tellin you, who cared bout them kids? Do you? With all them kinda things to worry bout, and hungry people can be mean people, most of em left there early as they could, goin to find some way to work and eat and live.

I remembers Dora saying all her life how she loved heat. Couldn't stand cold. Said she would never be warm enough after all them cold years of growin up. She almost always had some food in her hand or near her, too.

Dora decided to run away one day, when she was bout fourteen or fifteen years old. Musta been thinkin bout it a long time tho. Told me she had been lookin round to see how could she take care herself.

Everybody knows there is always some men, old and whatever, that be pokin they fingers and eyes toward girls they hope is too young to have any sense to know zackly what they is after. But, bein poor in close quarters like Dora had done grown up doin, she knew . . . what they was after. Some sense is just born in some people. Some without it, too. I know you knows.

Dora wasn't ugly and she wasn't dumb, I done tole you that. She sat and calclated a while on the mens in this town, old and young. The man she wanted had to have a place to live and a job. That liminated whole lot of the few that was. Her mind finally settled on one she thought was a nice man, cause he use to buy her little cheese and things when he be comin home from his work and see her standing staring in the grocery window. Name Larris. She decided to watch and see where he lived so she could talk to him. She did that.

One night she bathed good as she could with no soap, just rubbin her hands over them soapy tin holders in the shower. Pressed out her little clothes with her hands, then dressed and got in her cot with her clothes on. After the lights went out, she went out too.

Now, Larris. Larris was a nice middle-age man. Well . . . he was bout thirty-four or thirty-five. That's young now, old then, cause they was more tired. His wife had died not too long ago, I don't know from what cause, it's so many things a poor woman can die from. Her mama had took the two children to raise and Larris was alone in a nice little shack he had whitewashed clean, built a little fence around it while his wife was livin, cause he was a jealous man. He took care himself with a small job at the only railroad stop within about thirty-five miles round. He didn't do much and nothin important, but somebody got to keep things clean and do things nobody else want to. He did.

She got to his house, knocked on the door, didn't waste no time.

Said, "You got company in there with you?"

He was a little bewildered, said, "No. What's the matter?"

She asked, "Can I come in then? I wants to talk to you, Mr. Larris."

He didn't move, just frowned. "Me? Why? What's the matter?"

She went on round him and went in, lookin round to see did she want to live there. Turned back to him and said, "I know you been lookin at me . . . and I needs a husband."

He laughed, hand still on that open door. Laughed cause that was funny and he didn't have much fun in his life either now.

She asked him, "What you laughin at? You don't like me?"

He answered with a smile, "Course I like you. But I don't know you."

Dora said, "Well, you always buyin me things to eat, lookin at my dress tail."

He laughed again, said, "You always look hungry. And," he shut the door, "you got a nice lookin dress tail. Little ragiddy, but it's nice." He looked round the room, like she was doin. "Whyn't you sit down?"

She didn't laugh, said, "My dress tail is clean . . . and it ain't been nobody else's." She looked in his eyes to see did he get her meaning. He did.

"Little girl, what you know bout things such as that?"

Dora's stomach growled. Larris jumped up to get somethin for her. Said, "You hungry right now. I blive I got some . . ."

She stopped him, "I don't want nothin right now. What I want is to know what you gonna teach me if I be your wife."

He looked at her thoughtfully and sad-like. "You a child, girl. What you know bout love?"

She looked thoughtful and sad too. "I know I ain't got none."

He frowned, but didn't say nothin.

She went on, "I don't blive you got none neither."

He looked into her eyes. "That don't make you know nothin bout no love."

She say, "I know love makes babies."

He say, "It's more to love then that. People sposed to fall in love and try to be happy."

She say, "Let's fall in love then. Let's us try to be happy."

He laugh. "Girl, you can't just haul off and fall in love anytime you feel like it. If you make yourself fall in love, it won't last noway."

She smile. "Why? We sure can try. Let's us try." He didn't say nothin, so she went on. "I'm a clean girl, woman. I ain't never let nobody put they hands on me. I need a home. . . . And I want to fall in to that kinda love . . . wit you."

Larris looked just as deep in her clear young eyes as he could, as serious as he could be. Dora was kinda powerful when she got to talkin to you serious. She was makin him think bout somethin that hadn't even crossed his mind a hour ago.

She looked back in his eyes just as serious, and talkin. "Don't you want no children?" There was fear, as well as longing in her voice.

He smiled and answered, "I got two."

"Where are they then? You done give em away?" Fear in her eyes now.

He laughed, sadly, understandin. "Naw . . . they live with they grandmama."

She relaxed and smiled. "Ohhhh. They grandmama." She could almost taste the word. She remembered she was alone. "I could take care of em for you. You want your children back?"

He leaned his head toward her. "You just a child. What you know bout takin care of children? You ain't even been to no school. Can you read?"

She leaned her head toward him. "That's what you

want? Me, to read to you? Then, I'll learn. I can cook if I got food. I can clean up if I got soap. I can sew a little if I got a needle and thread. I done tole you, I'm a woman."

Larris smiled with half his face. Thinkin to himself, he spoke out loud. "Wellll . . . I been thinkin bout gettin me a woman of my own. I spected to get me one older than thirteen, fourteen years old tho . . ."

Quickly, Dora said, "I'm fifteen goin on sixteen."

Larris smiled, again, this seem to be his night for more smiles than he had in a year or so. "You mighty small . . ."

Dora smiled. "Big enough for you to see my dress tail."

Larris stopped smilin so hard. "What your mama and daddy gonna say?"

Dora stopped smilin. "I say for me . . . from now on."

Larris looked down into the bright, serious, hungry eyes set in a face that was smooth, clean and open honest. He knew the child needed everything and was tryin to survive. He began to respect her as more than a child . . . and we all know love is born in respect.

In one week, Dora had a new dress and a thin engagement band that would be the only weddin band she would ever have. Larris talked to Dora a whole lot. Told her he had two rules. Number one, no lovin til they was married so they would have no trouble. Number two, she would get the test of keepin, savin and spendin his pay one week, if she passed that and she could do it right, that would be settled. She would be the woman of his house. Equal to him as he was the man of the house. Now with a view back on all the men I done known and know to be known, he was a good, fair man. Then he smiled down at her from his man's perch! . . . respected her some more and thought the test would be too much for her, be failed by her and everything would be over soon. But . . . she passed the test. Both of em did.

Larris smiled cause, by that time, he sure liked that little girl-woman. He broke his own rule number one. He made love to Dora to be sure she was a virgin. She was. He wasn't, but men is like that sometime. A lot.

Chile, they got married. He was a little bit happy and plenty scared she might grow up and learn life and leave him, you know. She, Dora, heaved a great big sigh of relief . . . and grinned many days and nights startin out her marriage, her life. Mrs. Larris. She was the woman of his heart and life all the days of his life, which I know now, was only ten years.

Dora and Larris really did fall in love. They seem to be happy. I know she was. She was full all the time now. She was clean, she had clothes and that little ole house was her home. She blonged to somebody and somebody blonged to her. She musta been satisfied, cause she didn't go to lookin for her old family. I know she thought of em, but she didn't do no searchin for em.

Still, even with all that lovin, it was bout five years fore Dora had her first child. They turned out to be all girls. The first time, when she was pregnant, Larris told her she could name all the girls, he would name the boys. She said she was gonna name em all after herself, so everybody would know she had a family. Now! He thought she was just kiddin and he laughed. But she wasn't kiddin.

She was still in love, so the first daughter was named Lovedora. Little over a year later, the second daughter was named Windora. Cause, she said, her mind was more on gettin somewhere in this world than it was on love. Little over a year later, the third daughter was named Endora. Cause, she said, there wasn't gonna be no more. That one was the end. She was still happy to look up and see Larris comin home, cause she liked to say that word, "home." But I think the work of three children and all the washin, cleanin and cookin everyday, everything bein the same everyday, was kinda wearin her out.

Larris was always workin hard too. He was a sure-nuff steady, hard workin man. A good man. Tryin hard to take care his family. I think he was happy too. That's why it was so bad when he had that accident. See, one day on his job a foolish mistake was made bout a train backin up. He got a leg ripped off! Ohhhh, that poor man. His leg was gone! But that man, knowin all who was dependin on him did everything he could to get up and get back on his job. He knew he had to get well! Cause who was gonna take care them four people of his family? His medical attention left a whole lot to be needed. Them companies didn't help nobody much back then. And didn't want to give him no money to help him over! None!

Larris got well as he could and forced himself on back to work, tryin to do it on a crutch! They let him. Finally Dora hustled round them company offices and got him a peg leg . . . cause he needed that job. Now, that man loved his family, plus the two his mama was keepin, and he even still loved his job. Times was hard! But that man held up, with Dora's help, of course. She was workin at odd jobs she could do at home. I blive that's when she started cookin for people to eat at her house, holdin up them weak ends of they life. His backbone didn't crack and hers didn't neither, for no weakness to come sneakin out.

Chile, ain't life somethin?! Lord, oh, lord. Wasn't too long fore the same accident happened again to Larris, and he lost the other leg and a piece of his peg leg. That peg leg look just as sad as his real leg layin there mongst the tracks and gravel, dirt, rocks and blood. Was a man's life layin there! Cause he gave up, his mind just couldn't take it no more. Been tryin too hard to scuffle to get by, that's all they was doin . . . gettin by. He just hollared one of them men's deep, harsh screams whilst he was lookin down at the pieces of his body. While he stared at em, reachin for em like a wild man, his heart gave up . . . and died. And Dora would never smile down the street to see her man comin home to her again.

Dora grieved in what little time she had. Didn't have much time then cause she had to get to work. She be grievin, sometimes, as she be workin, but she also be makin plans for her daughters. Six, five and four years old. Dora was bout twenty-five years old then.

Now . . . Dora didn't have none of that false pride. She went right down there to the company and begged them railroad people. They didn't give her nothin, said it was his fault he died. Then she went to a lawyer she couldn't pay, offered him half of whatever she got. She wind up with $1500 of her own. The lawyer made them pay $3000. For a man's life! He sure musta been a good lawyer what wasn't in that railroad's pocket. In the meantime, they was survivin with Dora's cookin and washin for them workin mens. They come to her on accounta they knew what happened to her man.

When Dora got that money, she asked for cash. She just sit and stare at that money in her hands, count it over and over again. She didn't trust no bank. She stared at that money somethin awesome. She was a uneducated woman tryin to figure a way to make that money grow for her girls not to be poor someday. But everytime she count it, it still $1500.

In the end, all poor folks can come up with is the land. Land. Buy it. Couldn't afford to build on it, just buy it, hold it. Maybe grow somethin on it. So Dora went back to that lawyerman and he took her for a ride . . . to show her some land.

He pulled up, in his nice new little car, beside some land was covered with trash papers, empty bottles, little holes filled with muddy water. The land looked like it had bumpy, bad skin with a few whiskers here and there, little weeds, you know. Lawyer say she could get five acres for $200. apiece. Course Dora had told him what she wanted to spend. Ended up he owned that piece of land and they shoulda cost $25 a acre. But what did Dora know? She bought that land. One in each girl's name, two in hers. She slept with them deeds in her bed for bout two weeks, then she hid em in a rat-proof box and put em away. When she be close round where she hid it, she reach round, under and over something and pat that box, then go on back to work.

Dora's business now was cookin, feedin and washin for men who worked round the town what didn't have no wifes. So, she made a livin, fed her girls, worked em too, but kept em in school. And survived. Never wasted a dime. She had plans for her girls. Never did plant nothin on that land after just one time when all the plants died even with all her work on em. Land too hard and full of somethin wouldn't let them plants grow. It was too long a walk, too, for a tired woman to make every day. But, still, the land was there, the deeds in her box. Dora willed the town to move toward it, but it was slow.

I don't have to say times was hard early in this century. Everybody knows that, everybody what was poor. Didn't have to be no depression, things was just naturly depressed. Money was small. Things didn't cost much, cause if they did, nobody could of got them but the rich and that is mostly what was happenin anyway. So, people was glad to have what they Needed. Never mind if they got somethin they Wanted or not. NEED . . . that is what it is . . . what life is.

Now . . . Dora had been so taken-up in the girls and their livin, her emotions and things hadn't bothered her none. But, you know, they always do in the end, if you healthy, young or old, man or woman. Was one man was a customer. Not too old, not too young, round just right, I reckon. He was always starin at Dora as she put food out and took it in, talked to the mens, directed her children. Just stared at her. Well, she wasn't ugly. Neither was he, I must say. She sure was clean and strong and because her life was goin in somewhat a way she wanted, she felt good and she looked good. Them acres gave her comfort and confidence too.

That man, I done forgot his name, took to bein early at dinner. Dora be workin in her garden, you know she had one. He took to helpin out here and there, just friendly like.

Now . . . I don't know bout you . . . but spring can come and you be workin barefoot in that warm, damp dirt what feels good to you. All God's work be movin. You see a new plant comin up, a blossom for strawberries or a squash, anything. A new leaf. Feel the damp dirt after a light rain. Livin things growin and movin round you. Air full of birds and bugs. Dirt full of worms and other little bitty things, all of em movin, doin somethin. Life. And . . . things have a smell. They smell fresh. They smell like life.

I believe, unbeknownst to Dora, things was happenin like that, inside her. Remember, need is what life is. It's them needs that turns into wants, sometimes.

Anyway . . . he helped her . . . so he could watch her, I bet. He even brought a few flowers to plant, which she never did buy, needin food like she did. He helped and he never did want her to take nothin off his bill for his help. He took the little heavy jobs off her hands. Course, he enjoyed workin in the dirt too. It's somethin good and real about it, chile.

After a while, sometimes when he didn't come, Dora took to bein in the middle of standin, choppin, or weedin on her knees, and stop dead still, lookin out in the distance of the sky. Feelin the wind whippin lightly round her legs, her face, her breast. She became conscious she was still a young woman . . . and there was more to life then children and work. She began to feel her thighs rubbin gainst each other when she be walkin. Felt her body when she bend over or be reachin up or down.

At night, after they done got everything cleaned and put away, one of her daughters who all slept in one room, either Lovedora or Endora, usually leave their bed and go get in they mama's bed. Now, she sent them back sometime, when it rain. She lay there and listen to the rain beatin on the windows and the roof. She thinkin of life . . . of that man, you see.

Sometimes, she cry . . . and don't know why. She didn't realize she was lonely, you see. She thought she had too much to do to be lonely. Too many people around. But, I know, you can be lonely right in the middle of everybody in the world. Her tears didn't wash away that feelin of loneliness and sadness. And all the time, in her heart and tween her tired legs, the passion grew. Til . . . she began to think of him. Him.

One problem was, Dora knew this man didn't have nothin. Not even much as she did. She had a little home, a little business and five acres of land. And three growin girls. He probly had children, but she wasn't interested in that. Everybody could have a baby, they was almost free. He was poor. He, too, had been strugglin to survive in this here world all his life, even fore he left home probly. He didn't seem to have no roots, couldn't affort none. Had only a job what somebody could take anytime. She already been through that. She didn't want him. She didn't want to want him. But, she knew she wanted that man part of him.

I'm tellin you, you just fool round here and don't be watchin and ole life will just creep up on you! You be doin somethin you didn't plan! That must be why folks always be makin plans, tryin to see where they goin and what they doin!

One day, one rainy day again, he didn't go to his job for some reason. Head hurt, hand hurt, arm hurt, somethin. He came by to check on the garden. The children was in school. They was eight, seven and six years old then.

Dora opened the door without knowin it was him. She was not prepared to see her passion-man like that. The sky behind him so dark with thick, black clouds seem to push him through the door. The tree in the yard seem to have open arms, tellin her somethin, pushin him in. Was no bird sayin a thing. Just silence in the sound of the rain on the house, on the ground, in her heart. He smiled. She let him in. The little wailin sound in her throat as she opened her arms and took him into them, as he folded his arms around her, was drowned out by the tearing of a cloud by the lightnin. The thunder thundered and shook that little house. Her passion blew open like a volcano and shook her little body.

The time, the sounds, the rain, the silence, the passion, the touches, the thrills, turned into the lovemaking. And such a lovemaking it was!

When he finally left, before the children came home, Dora closed the kitchen. Wasn't gonna work no more that day. She went back to bed and just lay there, turnin her face to that rainy window and thought, thrilled, dreamed and slept til that next mornin when her normal life returned.

I think Dora should have got up and cleaned up, cause she soon found out she was pregnant. I tried to talk her into havin a abortion, but she wouldn't. So nine months later she had another baby girl. Because the gettin of this baby was so splendid, she named her new daughter Splendora. She loved the baby, but she didn't love the man anymore. She wouldn't even feed him when he wanted to pay. She let him go. Real Life was back with its ugly constant needs . . . and he was poor.

I thought she shoulda kept that man. You can sleep with money, but it don't make no thunder and lightnin passion, chile. You got to have a live human body for that. I sure did believe that! In my bones!

Now, her other daughters didn't like her havin that baby. As they grew up they always counted Splendora as a kind of outsider, you know? Not one of them, cause they knew their father was dead and he couldn'ta made that baby. As they grew up they sometimes told her she wasn't all part of them. They was jealous of their mother's love for her, too.

Anyway . . . Dora lived on, workin and takin care her girls she had such plans for, dreams for. I have a snapshot, a picture of Dora's house. Over the years the whitewash washed off in the stormin winds and rains. It was soon gray. Some loose planks stickin up and out. Porch a little tilted. Spokes gone from the porch rail. Fence leaning, somehow held up by strong bushes and plants Dora had set in. Some of them spokes gone too.

On the tiltin porch, Dora is standin, young, but leanin over just a bit from work and early strain. Four daughters in a row. Their hair is not straightened, just natural, but combed and brushed, rolled around rags so that they are smoothed, pulled back into soft rolls and pompadours. Tight curly knots at the start of a smooth long neck, pulled tight over tiny delicate ears, no earrings there. Arrow winged black eyebrows over black round and almond eyes that seem to look so deep into the camera, forgetting to smile, all cept Splendora. All lookin into somebody's camera like they tryin to see into the future. All of em had the same material dresses, gray blue with faded rose flowers in it, a bit raggedy, but clean. Windora's sewed hers a bit different, kinda stylish and all. But they was all long, to the ankle. No shoes, barefoot. Arms hangin straight down, all cept Splendora. Hers folded cross her chest. Her chest of small buddin busts that in a few years would be full and round.

165

It seems to be evenin time in the picture, or it's my dim eyes, or the gray of time. But I see the girls in that picture and they true . . . they true to life. I see the eyes of what each thought. They was all serious, but I know which way every one of them went. Course I was busy havin babies, right and left. I loved my man and he loved everybody. I didn't have all his children. But I loved him and I had all that he gave me. I got loaded down with children. They grown and gone now, and . . . I ain't got up yet. But, just like I watched mine, I watched them Doras.

Anyway, long with that cookin, Dora took to doin day work for the lady what owned the only little dress shop in town. We had a small partment store, but she carried the nicest dresses for the ladies had more money to spend. I don't know when Dora slept, guess she tried to stay way from a bed. But I be up runnin round town lookin for my man and his paycheck and I see her lights on all time of night. She be in there sewin or workin on somethin. She taught all them girls to sew, cept Endora. Endora was lazy as they come.

She always tellin them girls, "We goin SOMEWHERE! You all gonna be somethin!" She paid close attention to her daughters, specially after Splendora came and her load was so heavy. She studied each one separate.

Dora knew that Lovedora was a languishin, soft-bodied, soft-minded child, did everything kinda slowly, her mind off somewhere in one of her daydreams. She was named right . . . she dreamed of love. She try to do whatever you tell her to do, and smile that lazy smile at you, but the thing was never all done. Somebody else had to finish it. She worked at things, but was never really in things, just at em. A gentle, quiet woman-girl, full of dreams. Dora have to try to talk sense to her bout mens all the time cause the men really liked her. She start taking company early, but she stuck to one man-boy what came to see her a lot. She seem to love everything. Dogs, cats, cows, horses, flowers, trees, dolls, pigs, people, just everything came in her sight, she came to love it. She cried easy if somethin was hurt. She always stoppin doin what she ought to be doin, to go off and hold and hug something what she thought needed her love.

Windora was a strong-willed girl. Watched and studied everything. Could do most everything and do it quite well if she want to. Kinda nervous type, always movin, doing somethin. She the first one started helpin her mama on some of her outside jobs. She was young, but she liked bein at the dress shop and at the tailor's where she could pick up the scraps of cloth for her mama, or herself to make doll clothes with. She ask questions bout everything. She talked a lot, but it had to be about something. Always kinda thoughtful, interestin talk.

She look at the magazines at the dress shop and when they chance to give her a old one to play with, she guard it with care til she get to the tailor's, then ask him all them questions bout how to make them things for her dolls. Yea, she had dolls, she and her mama made em. She had paper-dolls too, she made them herself. Drew them dolls and cut em out, then drew clothes and colored em for them dolls too! She had lots of em. She like to make things. She had a bank what she kept hid, even from her mama. Put coins in it somebody outside had give her. Didn't spend em. Her mama talked to her bout money and business.

Endora was the kind of sickly one. I think she was puttin

167

on most the time cause she hate to do anything. None of em didn't hardly get to go to school them early days, but they went when they could be spared, which Dora liked to see was often as possible. I think Splendora was bout six or seven years old when Dora made a greement with the teacher in town, who had done gone blind, to clean her house in exchange for two more hours a day to teach her girls extra things, make em study. She said she couldn't feed no fools. But she couldn't keep that extra work up too long, so she stopped, and the teacher stopped all cept for Splendora. Splendora had done made a friend! And she really loved that blind teacher, did a lot of nice things for her. They all musta learned cause they could all read and cipher pretty well. Sure could count money and they even taught they mama to read a little too!

Endora was a pretty, smooth-skinned girl. Liked to eat, didn't like to work. The days she cooked, didn't nobody want to eat, but they had to, cause they was hungry. She was the one, there usually is one, the other girls joined hands against. But Endora didn't give a damn. She just lay cross a bed and rest, sulkin. Her mama always talked to her bout bein poor and findin a good strong husband, but Endora didn't pay boys no mind.

Now, these were all nice-lookin girls, gonna be good-lookin healthy women. But Splendora was splendid. Splendid.

The girl look like somebody drew her. She was built that perfect. She had a glowing, smooth skin. Long, fat hair braided into thick braids restin on her strong little shoulders. Strong, straight back, she never seem to slouch. Serious girl, thinking child, watched everything til she understood it, then she seem to forget it. She had them piercin eyes when she look at you. And when she asked questions they was never dumb, so you knew the answer better be good. I paid her special mind cause you had to bring your mind with you when you did anything with Splendora. Her mama talk to her bout all of life she knew. Bout what love was and wasn't. Bout money and the kind of freedom it most gave you. Bout God. Bout mens, all kinds and all colors. Don't know how Dora knew, spendin all her time workin like she did. Sure wish she hada talked to me fore I picked the wrong one to love.

I was talkin to Splendora and Lovedora one day, bout my man. Dora stopped me, said, "Don't tell them bout that thing you married to, he ain't worth a conversation. If you have to, then tell them what's wrong with him, not what you gonna make out of him, someday!"

I loved him, so I said, "He my husband! He a man."

Dora had a hard laugh sometime, she used it then. Said, "He another child of yours. He need whippin."

I say, "I can't whip him. If I do, he lose his manhood. And he got to have some manhood about him and all."

She say, laughin hard and low again, "He look out for his manhood well enough not to need you to do it for him. His manhood is his problem and yours too! I don't even want my daughters to know such a kinda manhood. They goin somewheres sides out in the streets to look for some man." She looked over at Lovedora who had done perked up to hear harder. "Least, I sure hope so." She ended.

All in all, Dora had some high hopes and big plans for her girls, or Dora Dolls, as she called em. She worked hard, hard til she was lookin old early herself. Sun-up to sun-down and some thru the night. She grew old and they grew up. You sure got a job to do if you got four pretty girls to watch over as they growin up. Sides keepin them full and clothed so they don't need nothin from somebody would take advantage of em. Sometimes it's more than two people can handle. Dora had to do it . . . alone.

That photograph picture I got of all of em on the porch of that house what was kind of run down? I blive is the last one of all of em together on that porch, and the last one of them together for a long, long time to come.

When Dora came down a little sick, her back in pain from heavy liftin and long bend-overs, Lovedora was bout eighteen years old. Not married yet cause her mama wouldn't let her. She liked the boys, specially that one I told you bout. Her mama tried to keep her head full of dreams of going someplace in life, but Ken filled them little empty spaces and grew!

Dora told Lovedora, "You the oldest. It's your turn to go out in this world and try to find a way to help your sisters get to someplace in this world."

Lovedora smiled her sweet, lovin smile.

Dora's voice got hard. "I mean that you can't think bout no boys right now! We all need everything! Your three sisters got to find a way out of the house and this town. I want you to help find a way to prepare for them cause you the oldest. We countin on you!"

Lovedora smiled her sweet, lovin smile.

Now, I can only tell you bout one of em at a time, cause they is four of em.

Me? Well, you know I had my family. I was kinda a bed and breakfast woman. Get in bed, make love, make babies, get up and cook, wash, iron, clean, garden, cause we sure needed that extra free food, then get in bed and start all over again, gettin to breakfast and all that work again. I was tired, but I sure thought I was happy cause I didn't know what else to think. I did think Dora was kinda crazy, pushin her children like that. I laughed at them . . . goin SOME-WHERE! Ha.

But anyway. . . . So that's how Lovedora went and got started.

<hr>

LOVEDORA

"You can wash, cook, clean, read, add, subtract, speak well, walk, run, and more. You healthy and clean. I got you a job as a clerk over at that dress shop. Don't pay much but you ain't makin nothin now! You can start there, learn all you can. When your next sister in line gets to work, we save all our money and maybe one day we have us a swell shop of our own. Windora can sew beautiful. Endora can do somethin! We goin somewhere. All we got to do is work . . . together." Lovedora had listened, her mama's words was ringin in her pretty ears as she bathed and dressed in one of Windora's own dresses she had made. Her sisters watchin her, smiling. Gettin ready to get over.

On that bright Monday morning she started out to work. But work was really not on her mind. She wanted to get married. They had already done planned it. Her and that boy, Ken. His family had a farm and they was gonna live there and work on that farm cause that boy said he couldn't leave his mama and papa, he bein the only boy-child. He was needed. She saw his need better than she saw her mama's. Ain't children somethin!?

But, still, Lovedora tried to do what her mama wanted her to. She always tried to do what people she loved say. She worked in that store bout two weeks. She did alright . . . but she was always dreamin of that Ken she was goin to marry. They was always talkin, too. He was always, after his work of course, leanin on a buildin not too far away from her job, or standin cross the street from it. She run out every chance she get, to talk to him. They kept makin them plans, chile, til Lovedora quit that job and ran off on her payday, bought her own weddin ring and married that man on the same day! She saved some money out for Dora, tho, and gave it to her when they stopped by the house to tell her. Lovedora was too romantic to be scared of her mama.

Dora was so stunned off her feet, all she could do was sit down, drop her lips open and stare at them children, wonderin what she had done wrong. She hadn't done nothin wrong, just everybody got they own mind to deal with. And what anybody gonna do bout love?

Dora try to say it ain't love, just romance, and Lovedora would suffer for it. But Lovedora looked happy to me. When they left, Dora went to bed and stayed there for two days, cryin at the waste, she said. Anyway, Windora got sent down to keep that job Lovedora walked off of. She seem glad to go! Wasn't no love on her mind. Just gettin ahead and out!

Lovedora and Ken was happy for a long time. Bout two or three years. Didn't no children come. Both Dora and Ken's mama and papa was glad bout that. But the man, Ken, started changin.

See . . . Lovedora did love everything. She loved all the animals on the little farm. Specially the new born. She even took care his retarded sister, playin with her and, Lord knows, hadn't nobody taken up no time with that child in yearrrrs. They was all used to her and tired of that poor chile. But Lovedora cared for her. She took pleasure in it.

Lovedora ran, jumped, played round that farm til it look like she was havin a good time and lots of fun. That began to make that man annoyed and mad at her. She be laughin and he be tired and get mad. Well, he sure be workin in the hot sun on the hard land. His family was grudgin him his pay for bringin home a poor wife so early in his life, fore they could get all they could out of him, you see. They prayed she didn't get no babies, and that might be why she didn't, but she sure didn't. I wish somebody had prayed over me!

You all know what all a family can do to make your life miserble. In two, three years, he was miserble and he was makin Lovedora miserble too. She didn't understand why, cause she was still in love with love. She got sadder and sadder. Laughter got low or not at all. She stuck to the animals more, til his family thought she was a real sure-nuff fool. Ken took to goin out nights, even in his overalls, and comin home jumpin on that pretty child. Not too much, cause he was scared of Dora who walked over there every Saturday or so. Lovedora didn't tell her mama bout them whippins, so she couldn't get no help there. His mama didn't give a damn cause she had done taken her licks and still did sometimes. I think she was glad of em, myself.

Long with all the dirty work they could get Lovedora to do, was the walk to the road to get the mail. Now, there was a son-man who pass up that road sometimes goin to see his family who live cross the way from Ken's folks. He was a very nice-lookin man, but his looks didn't have nothin to do with his heart. He had a oldish, blue cadillac with a few dents in it, and he dress what look like nice in little cheap suits from our little cheap partment store. He walk real slow, always lookin over his shoulders to keep up with what's goin on round him. Lovedora loved his car cause it was blue, so he took to wearin plenty of blue when he take that ride to his folks. He always stop and talk to her, make her laugh, listen to her troubles, til she rush on back to her misery house. It got to be that bout every time Lovedora go to get the mail, he just be passin by. They talk some more.

He lean over toward her, his hat crooked on the side of his head, his arm restin on the seat top in such a way she couldn't see the split in the seams under his arm, his knees wide open neath the steerin wheel, wigglin a little. A smile that woulda broke his mother's heart could she see it, stead of that sad face he make when he ask his mama bout her money.

He say to Lovedora, "Sugah, what you need, a fine woman like you, is a real man to preciate you."

Lovedora say, sadly, "Well, my husband, I think he really try . . ."

"Darlin, I am too much of a man to say somethin bout another man, but I care too much about you not to tell you the truth. That boy you got for a husband, he don't know what to do with you! You are the cream of the crop. A queen! He don't know nothin bout no queens."

Lovedora grin, glad to hear somethin nice bout herself. "Ohhhh, you go on. I am not a queen. I'm just a woman who wants to be treated right."

He grins, showin them teeth what needs to see a dentist
. . . soon. "Baby, he don't know nothin bout life. He need
to grow up, be a man. Now me . . . I am a man. One of
these days, when you be thinkin like a sure-nuff serious,
grown-up woman, you gonna let me show you the world and
how it feels to have a honest-to-god real man that treat you
like the queen you is!"

Then Lovedora smile and walk real slow back to misery
house, thinkin.

She stuck with Ken bout a year more, til he came home
one night and abused her with his fists for no reason at all
cept she was full of love and didn't know how to be mean
back. Then he had sex on her and fell asleep. She got up in
misery in the gray morning, packed a little shoppin bag with
a few of her things and set out walkin back to her mama.
She did kiss the retarded sister good-by, and took whatever
little happiness that girl was gonna have in her life with her.

Now, I know that man did not just sit out there and wait
to see when Lovedora came out, but some kinda reason, he
was passin down that road that mornin. He came along
whilst she was walkin down the road, tiltin with carryin that
bag, and offered her a ride home. She accepted. But he
didn't take her to her mama's house, he took her to his room
on the main sportin street in town. All the way there he was
justa tellin Lovedora bout how long he had loved her and
what all they could do together now she had left that fool.

She just stared at him, big-eyed (one gettin black), and
she was in such a pitiful state of need in her heart, she just
shifted that love she had done had for Ken right on over to
Zero. They gave him that nickname in school because he got
so many of em. It wasn't but bout three days fore Lovedora

was not only livin on that street, but was walkin it, makin money for Zero so they could have their dreams.

She thought she was in love and didn't know what she was doin. I blive she was innocent in her heart. I hate to think that woman's head was empty. Cause, in time, that woman whored some, stole some, lied a lot to mens. She thought they was gonna have a life with the money they made together. She didn't have sense enough to see he wasn't makin NONE! He said he was goin to let his other woman go when they had enough saved. Only, he didn't save NONE. He just stand in front of that Town Bar, leanin on the wall watchin how many men his women caught. He spent that money gamblin and snifflin that dope, or whatever they do with it.

After the umpteenth time her mama had done been down there, threatenin to kill Zero, but she couldn't never find him!, she made Lovedora go home with her. Bathed her, fed her, stroked her, loved her and sure did talk to her with every stroke of wisdom she could find, and prayed over her. Lovedora went back down there to Zero cause she thought she loved him. Broke Dora's heart . . . again . . . and again . . . and again. She want to go back down to that street and shoot that Zero, but I talked her out of it. Told her, "You can't go round killin people! Your daughter done made up her own mind bout that man! You can't shoot him! Do . . . you gonna have a bigger sin on your hands!" Yes, I told her that. Me!

It had been three years her first daughter had been in sportin life. The others was doin alright, as alright goes, but the one you hurt the most for is the one who is hurtin! For Dora, that was Lovedora, then.

But I blive when somethin is in a child, it will have to come to the top just like cream. In time, things her mama had raised her on came to the top of her brain. It happened in another strange way. Of course, she fell in love again, that was just her way. Of course, her type of livin helped!

Nights with strangers slobberin, pawin all over you just cause they got ten or twenty dollars. Puttin somethin, so private it was the first thing Adam and Eve covered up, inside your body. Comin "home" so tired and dirty, maybe full of them little germs that mean dirty business eatin up your insides. Gettin beat up if you ain't got enough money for a man who ain't been doin nothin but talkin, laughin and throwin the money away what you go through all them things for. Puttin things in your mouth the good Lord saw sense in puttin tween somebody's else's legs. Lovedora did refuse to do that tho. Bein put out, in the middle of a dark, cold mornin, to get out and make some more money for some dope or somethin to gamble with! All for some nothin that don't care nothin bout you! And who respects you for bein a good money-maker? No! nobody. Not even him, who you make it for!

Lovedora woke up one mornin and she was miserble, miserble! Poor little thing, just want to love somebody . . . not everybody! Heart so big it pressed in on her brain . . . slowed it down. She didn't like sellin her body, it had been for Zero and their future. Her mama had taught her better, much better. Said, "Get somewhere in the world," not "Lay down for the world." And another thing happened. Ken, her ex-husband, came down to buy some of what he used to get free, from her. Zero called to Ken, and Lovedora heard him say to him, "Do what you wants to to the bitch. Just don't fuck with my money and don't put no marks on her, cause she got to work!" Wasn't he nothin!? I'm glad she heard him cause she was a wide-hearted woman gettin to be a wide-legged fool. Lonely, even with all them men jumpin in her.

Chile, It's somethin bout life, just somethin, will come along. You just got to make the right choice when it do. I musta missed mine.

Now . . . some of them men, truck drivers and such as come through town, is awful lonely in they real life . . . and need a woman. One day, one of them who always came back to Lovedora really fell in love with her! He talked to her everytime he made love to her, WHILE he was makin love, cause he read her heart. He made love realllll slow. It ain't nobody's business how I know!

Like I say, he talked to her whilst he makin love to her.

He wait awhile til it get good to him. He say, "In the bottom of your heart, you really my woman."

"I'm the one loves you. Gonna take care of you."

"I be . . . good to you."

"You KNOW . . . you blongs to me!"

"When you gonna . . . . seethetruth?"

"You my woman, Lovedora."

"Always.   ALWAYS."

"MINE.   All mine."

"Be GOOD   to you."

"Lovedora . . . I . . . am . . . your . . . true-man."

"Always   always   ALWAYS."

"Gonna . . . love you . . . love you . . . love you. . . . Always, baby."

"I'm . . . yours."

178

"Say you mine. Say it. Say it. SAY it. Tell me."

"Cause . . . I . . . I . . . I . . . I . . . . loveyouuuu."

Like that, he talk like that . . . and many more things too. My man talk like that to me sometime, but I was gettin tired of it, cause it always make me another baby.

Basil was his name. Basil bring her little presents. Treat her gentle, tell her stop goin with all them other men, givin his love away, sellin his love away. For what? He ask her that. And you know she didn't have no answer. She sure couldn't say it was for no Zero.

For the first time, Lovedora got pregnant, and she knew it was Basil's. And she wanted that baby . . . and her own man.

Soon after that, Lovedora woke that mornin after her mama had been down there again and Basil was back. She packed a bag again . . . in the middle of that night, and left. This time in a eighteen-wheeler truck. They stopped in front of Dora's place so she could tell her mama her life had changed, leave her some money and say good-by right.

Dora said, "Thank God. Thank God!"

Windora grunted genteelly in her pretty robe. She was gettin ready to leave for Chicago at that time.

Endora smiled, nobody knew why, cause you never knew what Endora was thinkin.

Splendora just hugged Lovedora and Basil til they left.

All their lives had been movin on, too.

Anyway, Lovedora left with her man. Got married and stayed with him and had four more babies with him. The first girl, she wanted to name so she could remember what she had gone through to get to her new happiness, so she thought of pain. Didn't want to name her *pain,* so she took the *i* out and named her Pandora. See, she had done found out she had TB by then. She had care, but she couldn't never get rid of that TB. See, a real housewife have a real job to do, and with four kids, it's a hard job. His love and care, her love and some medicine kept her well enough to be happy enough.

Basil was good as his word, he was good to her, he loved her. He gave her a home and fixed it nice for her and the children. She was always able to send a little money home to help Dora with the dreams.

They would be together now if he was still livin. He dead now. They was married a long time. Kids most grown. That Lovedora just had to have some love in her life. I wonder what she gonna do now? I blive she coming back home soon. See, he was sick a long time and it cleared out their savings and I blive she losin the house. So . . . she comin home.

Me? Well, round that time, soon after Lovedora had left, one of my own daughters went down to the street to sportin life. I went down there with my gun. I waited for the man who had put her out there, I found him and told him, "You better leave my daughter alone! If you got some sense."

He a smart aleck, said, "Ole lady, you can't tell me what to do with my woman!"

I'm smart too, said, "I can sure stop you!"

He dumb too, said, "Can't nobody take apart nothin I put together. Can't nobody take her away from me! Nothin can stop me doin what I want to do! And I wants her in the street." He turned to his friends and laughed.

I said, "I can stop you. I can put a bullet in your ass!"

Then I pulled out my .45 and pulled the trigger. Didn't care where I hit, I shot him.

He didn't laugh no more.

They took me to jail, but they didn't give me no time. They let me go. Dora came down to get me. Said, "Girl, you shot that man! You told me NOT to shoot the one had my daughter out there! Now, you got a big sin on your hands."

I told her, "Well . . . now I understand better what you was feelin. I might have the sin, but he ain't got my daughter no more!" And that was the end of that! My daughter came on home like she had some sense. Didn't nobody else on that street want her after that noway!

My husband, when he came home, told me, "You sure was a fool to go down there to that place and tangle with them mens! Who you think you is? A man!? You gon let these kids get you killed, woman! Don't look to me to make no fool of myself! Eh! Eh! Lord, look what I done got me! A fool for a wife!" He wiped his chin from the food I had just paid for and fixed him. "Gimme some money, woman. Let me get outa this crazy house."

For the first time, I didn't split what I had with him. I told him, "Get it where you slept last night!" And went on bout my business cleanin my house I paid the rent on.

Then, our lives moved on.

~~~~~~~

WINDORA

Windora started out and was workin out real well at the dress shop. She got to the place she was only there part-time

181

cause she was designin and makin her own things for other people. Some was even put in the shop she worked for. She was makin and savin money for her own shop one day, in a big city. She helped her mama and sisters too. She taught Endora and Splendora things to do for her work, so they learned too. Endora was still lazy. Her mama, Dora, told her she better keep her eye out for a man. "A man with his own business," she said. But Endora wasn't studyin no men.

Now! Windora had made some long plans for her life. Had been makin them for a long time. Some of em might have started when she was in school. It truly hurt her when she was in school and the other children laughed at her clothes. Called her "Poverty." But some of them wasn't much better off. Some of them was, cause it was only one grammer and junior high school here, mixed together. Some of em's parents had money tho.

She took to stayin to herself. Always standin by some window, lookin off into space dreamin of what she wanted to have. She read early, and a lot. Head always stuck in some book. She learned early to sew her own clothes and she always looked better than her sisters. She never dreamed of havin a husband, she dreamed of havin all the money she wanted. And she was a very clean child, bathed without bein told. I knew, without knowin how I knew, that Windora hated bein poor more than the others, and that hate she had spread out to people and things. Oh, she loved too, her mama, for instance. Maybe her sisters. Money, for sure. But she was pushed into herself, into life, into plannin and dreamin, by hate as well as love. Even so, I wished I had a daughter like her.

She made doll clothes, and doin that, she made a friend

mongst one of the little white girls whose parents had money. That friend used to invite Windora over to play with the dolls she made clothes for. Windora liked to be in that house. Used to ask for things, politely, of course, just to get a chance to see the servant do them. Liked the thick, satin drapes, the rich, soft carpets, the fires glowin warmly in the huge fireplaces, feelin the pretty material of the dresses in her friend's closet. She never woulda come home if Dora didn't send after her. She finally took to leavin early just to keep from havin them to see her poor-lookin sisters.

She liked music too. She fought her mama bout takin violin lessons. Dora didn't want to spend that money on no violin. Said they could all take the piano, then she didn't need to get no credit and debt cept for one instrument. But Windora helped her mama so much, she demanded and cried and wouldn't eat, til Dora got her that violin from the pawnshop. But Windora had to pay for her own lessons with the money she made from makin doll clothes for other kids.

She was glad when Lovedora got married and didn't keep that job at the dress shop. She was dreamin of that job. Like I said, she did well at it, even to startin to make her own money from her own clothes. The owner really liked Windora and her work. But Windora didn't plan on stoppin there any longer than she had to. She saved her money. She got in them contests for designin. She wrote them designin schools for scholarships and loans so she could go to their schools. She finally won somethin in Chicago and they was to help her get a job in a dressmakin factory. They didn't call it that, but that's what I call it.

She been doin all that while Lovedora was out on the streets. She hated her sister bein out on them streets and when she see her anywhere, she wouldn't speak to her, just pass Lovedora by like she had never done seen her in life! When Lovedora was leavin with Basil, Windora was glad. Now that part of her would not be in everybody's face. She thought Lovedora was a big failure. Anyway she soon left too, goin to Chicago! Splendora took over the job at the dress shop, but still kept some of her baby-sittin jobs. Endora said she was sick.

Windora got started in school and on her new job. She was serious bout both of em. They found her a place to live what they called safe. Windora was, also, a good-lookin, classy, reserved kinda woman. Kept to herself. Was still a virgin, even. Her boss, a nice gentlman, watched her work for two, three months. Watched who she went out with . . . nobody! At the end of that time, he started lookin at her designs she had never been to school for. He liked em. He started takin her to lunch so they could talk about her work. He knew she wasn't eatin too good either.

That man liked Windora. Windora thought she needed him. Now, he didn't plan it zackly, she did plan it zackly. They finally slept together, made love. Windora, bein a virgin, got his respect and some kinda love soon followed. She made love bout eight times with that man, tryin to get pregnant. She didn't zackly want no baby, just wanted a hold on somebody who could help her. After all, that virgin stuff had to be worth somethin, you just didn't throw it away! She got pregnant. Told him. Asked him at the same time for a special favor so she could take care herself better, without too much of his help, she said.

Windora wanted a corner in the buildin all to herself, to design her clothes, a place to make them and a showroom to show them. She got em! Plus, he added seamstresses to help her, save her time. Windora worked as hard as anybody could slicin out a place in the world for herself. She still kept livin in that safe room all the time she was pregnant. And she wouldn't make no more love. "Because I don't want to hurt the baby," she said.

When that baby was almost here, she made love one more time. She asked, then, for a nice apartment to bring their baby home to. She was doin fine with her work, just needed help gettin started, findin and furnishin a place. She never gave him no trouble with his family and things, so he helped her again. I make it sound so easy, but it took plenty plannin on her part, actin, workin, watchin, learnin to do the thing right. You know, still keep her business, have a future, live now and keep him too! Cause she wanted her own salon someday. She didn't mean to be workin for nobody long.

When her baby was born, yes, it was another girl. She named it Goldora. Dora came up to be with her awhile. She was soooo proud of one of her daughters makin it! Windora was goin SOMEWHERE! She was makin and followin her dream and, in the doin, her mama's dream. Dora came home glowin! She loved havin another "Dora" for a grandchild, too.

Round bout that time, my first daughter, who had been on the street for that man, was married and settlin down. But I had another daughter who was school-smart and wanted to go to college. We needed some money! That man of mine still wasn't always bringin his money home. I had done stopped chasin him for his love and finally for his money too. Got so I just couldn't find him, so I stopped lookin!

What made me so mad was, even when me and my kids work at things to make money for us to live and put some aside, he would find it and take it out the house too! We coulda helped my daughter get to college cause she had worked hard enough for a scholarship! But he didn't give a damn. So, I pulled my .45 out on him and told him to "Get your ass out of my life cause your ass is all that's in it. You take everything else somewhere else, so just take that empty-pocket ass of yours there too! We ain't needed you in a longggg time!" You know, that man cried?! Didn't want to go! Then I knew, Dora was right, I had married a fool. And he had to go!

After he left, all my kids and me worked hard, day and night, til my daughter was able to get on way from here to that college for to be a dentist. We all had a paper route, me too. Up at 4:30 A.M. rollin papers, then gettin out deliverin em. We sold everything we could get our hands on, door to door. We mowed lawns, we cut trees, we cleaned houses and garages. EVERYTHING! She is a dentist now. Smile, smile, smile. And she done sent her younger brother to college for to be a veterary what works with animals! All us at home got beautiful teeth. When she first graduated, I didn't have but eight or nine teeth left in my mouth! Now, I got a mouth full. When I look in the mirror and smile at myself, which I do all day, I love my teeth. Cause my daughter made em, chile!

When I put my husband out, tho, Dora said, "Oh no! Not you! You told me havin a hot-flesh man was better'n nothin, even a poor one who didn't have nothin but that thing crouched tween his legs!" I laughed, but when I got home, I cried.

Anyway, Windora took to sendin money home to help her mama for her dreams. She sent clothes home too, cause she knew they didn't have much to do nothin with. The one bad thing for her was she was losin her eyesight. Been sewin by bad light for so many years. She could see her child tho, she watched her close. She started havin big plans for Goldora too, but we'll get to that.

Now, I know it sound like she didn't have much struggle. But she did. She was scared sometime in that big city. Well, you got to be. It's natchel, if you got sense, cause everything in the world is there. People who got everything and people who starvin to death. Just happen it turned out mostly like she planned. Bein a virgin helped, it set her apart from bein a gold digger, the man thought. It made her pure in his sight. He really would have done more, but she was careful not to ask too much. When she didn't want to have sex anymore, he thought it was just the goodness in Windora comin out. It was really just that she didn't feel like it with him nor nobody else she knew. She was tired. And it hadn't got good to her. So she just used sex when she needed to. That's sad, ain't it?

You just know she finally got her own shop. Wasn't no hi-falutin place in no spensive place. Just a nice, nice shop with some beautiful clothes in it. She had good customers and they came regular. She made it. She was raisin Goldora very well, gettin her ready to go to college. Had already been sendin her to private schools! Just wasn't no love in her life. And she was goin blind. Her glasses was awful, awful thick now. She was lonely too, like she never thought she would be.

The men she let take her out, all of em had somethin goin for them in a business way. Or they was professional mens, doctors, lawyers, stuff like that. But, no matter what Windora thought she wanted, she had been raised by down-to-earth humans, and most of the men she knew was what you call phony. Wantin things so other people could know they had em, not just cause they enjoyed em theyselves. Windora was more real than they were! So she didn't fall in love with em. She just got tired and unhappy.

I blive she's comin home soon now, too. I know Splendora is, and she done told everybody she want to see em, be there! Chile, that Splendora is splendid.

Me? You know, I use to think Dora pushed them kids to do too much. After my dentist daughter, I understood bout school pushin. But she wanted them to be too clean, too nice, too mannered, to dream. Dream. Try most anything to get SOMEWHERE. I thought she was too hard on em. But now, I don't know. I just lost a son from a overdose of them drugs. I couldn't help him and I couldn't stop him. He gone. Just gone.

And I got a daughter who drinks every minute she awake. Mens just take advantage of her, she don't get no money and no respect. Sure ain't gonna get no husband again. Why was they so unhappy they turn to death . . . away from me? Away from life? Was it cause they didn't have no dreams?

I don't know, I just don't know.

At least Dora's children is still livin. No matter if they sick and blind, they livin! I want you to know I was in pain,

I am in pain, from my kids' pain. And I'm tired. If it wasn't for my dentist and my veterary, I'd just want to die, cause I wouldn't be able to see nothin I had done with my life. Is that what Dora meant?

But . . . anyway.

ENDORA

Now . . . Endora was lazy, but she wasn't no fool. She knew if she kept livin at home, she was goin to have to work. She didn't want that, and didn't care too much bout goin "somewhere" either. She had her own plans.

Most of her young life had mostly been turned into herself. She didn't pay no mind to what other people thought of her or her clothes or her bare feet. She had liked the piano when the lessons was goin round. For some reason she liked to play at funerals instead of weddins. She didn't like death, just that everybody was busy so didn't have reason to hold her up in no conversations.

She liked nice clothes, just didn't take no bother to keep hers up, so she was always sneakin Windora's or even Splendora's things, dressin outside and goin on from there. One thing, she did like to cook! But not for no big ole group of people, just a few, like her family. She wanted to invent new dishes, play around with the recipe. Her things came out good, too! Sometimes.

Anything she didn't want to do, she got sick. She didn't mind stayin in bed for days if she had to. Sometimes she had to, cause that's the way Dora punish her if she say she was sick.

She was a thin, willowy, rose-stem kind of girl. Serious, less she be talkin to Lovedora when she was still home. People tell her bout fellows what liked her, she just say, "Phuwee!" or somethin like that. She like sports, long as she runnin the game. She read some, not much, just enough to be too busy to work, less she found a real special sexy book. I know, cause she traded them with my daughter that drinks a lot.

Endora stumbled upon what she was gonna do with her life, you might say. She loved them cherry cokes they had down there at the little black drugstore. She be goin down there all the time, just a'sittin, lookin at all goin on round her, for hours. Never woulda come home if she hadn't been sent for. Everybody knew where she was! But didn't nobody know why she was always there. But me. I found out. Just a way I got, I guess.

There was a cute little ole womanish girl worked there, at that soda fountain, named Belle. Now, Belle was cute as a bug's ear! She just be makin them ice cream things and all kinda cokes, justa twistin and turnin, lookin cute. Had a real plump, nice shape. That's who Endora liked to talk to. Who she liked to stare at, be around. I don't think she knew why, at first. But she always got mad at the boys and men who hung around there tryin to get close to Belle. Talk smart to em, didn't like em, even if they try talkin to her own self!

She was always tellin Belle, "What you let all them men talk to you for? They don't want nothin worth nothin."

Belle laugh and say, "Oh, I don't know that what they want ain't worth nothin! I think it is!" Then Belle turn to somebody she waitin on, say, "You want whip cream or ice cream on it?"

Endora snap her head up in the air, "Humph! I wouldn't let em say nothin to me! You too good for them! You can do better than them!"

Belle fizz up some coke syrup and stir, say, "With who? Who you know that I don't know about?" Then she turn and ask somebody, "Want a straw in it?"

But then Endora don't say nothin else, cause she don't know for sure who she talkin bout. All she know is she like to touch Belle's hand, hold her arm if they happen to walk down the street together. Watch her hips when she be turnin in that little small space behind that counter. She knew she wanted to touch Belle's breasts. She loved breasts. Everybody's! She didn't have much at that time herself. So that was her favorite thing to do . . . watch Belle. Belle had big busts, big hips, big legs and a big mouth. She love to see Belle turnin and sayin, "You want whip cream and a cherry on top?"

As she grew older, she came to herself. When she be layin in bed at night pattin on herself like some people do, she think of Belle, then she be shamed and not know why she think of Belle. She just didn't like no boys. She just told herself one day, "I want Belle." Then she commence to really sittin on that stool at Belle's counter every spare minute she could find and all day Saturday. Belle thought they was good friends. I blive Belle would have accepted Endora if she had really known what Endora was feelin, but her brain was lightweight. She didn't know for a long time.

Now just to splain a little so you will understand what happened, let me tell you bout the druggist man. He had been married bout fifteen years to a very uppity woman who didn't want him in the first place. She spent all his money, drank a lot of his liquor, givin a lot to her friends too. She was a alcoholic person. Drunk or sleep most the time. Or just not there where he was. Gone! He never got no lovin or treatment like he thought he deserved. As time went by, he quit beggin his wife so much and went to starin at Endora. She was fresh and good-lookin and always in his store. He thought she might be in there to watch him, cause sometimes she did watch him a long time as he waited on his customers. Anything to keep from starin at Belle all the time, once she knew why she was starin. She didn't want the fellows comin in there to get the right idea either.

So, it came to be that a romance blew up where there really was none at all. Then Endora began to take pleasure in teasin him with her eyes. She smile and look away, like she shamed to get caught lookin at him. He liked that, cause hadn't nobody paid him no mind in a long time.

They flirted, I mean they flirted hard. He commence to givin her things, playin like he was goin to throw them away anyhow. She took em. That way, Dora got to have a lotta soaps, bubble baths, cheap perfumes, aspirins, mouthwash, cheap earrings, bracelets, makeup for Splendora, all them kinda things they got in a drugstore.

Then, fore Windora left town, Endora began to steal her clothes, pretty clothes, to wear for a afternoon sittin down on a stool lookin at Belle, while the druggist was lookin at her and she awardin him a look and a smile every once in a while. When she leave to go home, she always back out the store lookin at him, but talkin to Belle. He got her last look every time with what he thought was a little tiny smile, but what was really a smirk. I blive that's what they call em, smirk, when somebody's laughin at you!

I hope I ain't got to tell you how many fools there is in this here world! That man started plannin on how to get rid of his wife. He finally offered her whatever she wanted if she would just go! She really wanted to go, but she wanted enough money to keep her in Jack Daniels for the rest of her life and it look like she might get it! But that man put a detective on his wife. Whatever he found, and I knew it was plenty, it worked. He was soon free.

Bout that time, Belle was gettin awful close to one of them fellows was always hangin round and Endora got mad. She quit goin in the store so much. She keep usin Windora's clothes tho. Windora was screamin bout how come her clothes always be dirty and she just be done cleaned em up! Nobody say nothin cause nobody really knew cause Endora dress away from home.

Endora put them clothes on and walk and walk all over that town. She began to like them soft, flowin, drapin clothes. Nothin too tight. White or soft pretty prints. Look pretty on that rose-stem body of Endora's. Stolen white pearls in her ears and round her neck. Some people born knowin what's right for what they want to do. So now, besides wantin Belle, she want some money too!

Mr. Nile, the drugstore man, missed her when she stop comin in so much. Thought his presents wasn't big enough for her after all. When she was in the store, he took to slippin her some money. He musta been overchargin all these poor people to be able to pay off his wife and give Endora some money too, and still keep up his own bills, store and all! That man was spendin money!!

Then, too, Endora was thinkin she was kinda sickly and she might need somebody with some medicine as a friend for a long time. She start goin back into that store for them cokes she didn't have to pay for no more, wearin all her borrowed finery, every chance she got, and stare at Mr. Niles.

Never take her eyes off him, now, for at least a hour or such. She had to get home quick sometime, case Windora get there first. Windora was takin more time off now, gettin ready to leave for Chicago. Still, everytime Endora leave, she back up real slow to the door, lookin at him all the time. No smile, just a deep, deep look.

If you wonder why I know so much, Hell! I had to watch! I was raisin girl children. I was learnin somethin too!

Anyway . . . Mr. Niles and Endora had not never talked with nothin but their eyes, but, chile, twenty minutes after that man got his final papers, Endora was sayin, "I sure do." Well, she sure did! That chile knew what she was doin . . . but he didn't.

He was so excited! I'm glad he didn't have to mix no medicine, cause somebody sure woulda died that night! He carried her over the doorsteps, holdin her close in his arms. She justa smilin up at him, holdin him round the neck. He went on through the livin room, straight to the bedroom. He laid her gently on the bed. She smiled up at him. He kissed her cheeks, her lips when he could find em, her ears. She smiled up at him. He turned off the lights and undressed. He couldn't see her smile no more.

He reached under her dress. She frowned, said, "What you think you doin?"

He smiled down at her through the darkness he could see in now. "You my wife now."

She kept frownin. "So? What that mean? That you can haul my body round ever which way you want to?"

He smiled, only a little now. "You my wife. We sposed to do this . . . darlin."

She shook her head slowly, "No," said, "Ah annh! We did not ever court. We got to court now. You got to win me. . . . Like a prince or somethin in books. Bein your wife just makes it more convenient, that's all. I want to be courted . . . and won . . . by my husband." That child sure was lazy. Or smart!

That man got up. He wasn't smilin. It was dark, but he saw the light. Said, "What have I got here? You been makin up to me with all those smiles, all this time. Now you . . ."

She innerupted him. "I'm smilin at you now, darlin." She smiled in the dark. "But you have to show me how much you love me. Make me want to . . . give all my love to you . . . my virgin body. Court me. Then . . ." Her voice trailed away. Mr. Niles huffed and puffed, but he didn't blow Endora out.

Mr. Niles began to court his wife, Mrs. Niles. Many trips, diamonds and fur coats, much champagne (she read about that at the magazine rack in the drugstore) and many, many dresses, suits and coats she bought from her sister . . . later, she let him make love to her. She was a virgin, he was pleased. Endora was still lazy. She didn't let him make a lot of love, but her timin was good. It was just enough lovin to keep him huffin and puffin after his own wife. He lost weight and frowned a lot, but he kept her.

While all that was goin on, Endora talked quite a bit to

Belle. See, now she could hire and fire people who worked there. When she sittin there sippin on somethin, Belle quit spendin too much time talkin to them fellows sittin round there. The light had done turned on in her brain. When, one day at closin time, Endora looked her in the eyes and smoothed her hands cross Belle's breast? Belle looked her straight back in the eyes, said, "You want whip cream or ice cream on it?" And they went on from there. It ain't none of my business, so I can't tell you nothin bout it. I do know Belle had the most prettiest uniforms I ever done seen, but I ain't been nowhere! And she could almost tell Mr. Niles what to do, now!

I don't blive, in fact I know, Dora don't know nothin bout all that. Why should she? She don't need to know. And Endora must didn't make herself like that, cause for a long time even she didn't know bout herself. Dora was wantin her daughters to go off from this town and get SOMEWHERE in life, but she thought Endora had done pretty good for herself, so she was satisfied.

Life just move in on you if you ain't watchin it. Cause you all know a triangle such as that wasn't gonna bring nothin but trouble some day.

Anyway, Endora was now able to help her mama with the last dream at home. At least, she gave her money now and then, and kept her supplied with everything they carried in that drugstore! She bought lots of her clothes from her sister Windora, helpin her. She bought from other big stores too, out them fashion books. She traveled a lot, takin Belle with her sometimes, she might be gone a month. Takin Mr. Niles with her, she might be gone a weekend or a week. Said the store couldn't do without him. I don't think he ever missed his first wife, but I blive he knew he was missin somethin!

As the years passed, Belle began to almost run that store, cause she was kinda runnin Endora. She did the hirin. She hired the wrong girl one day, cause Betina was a pretty little ole young girl and Endora began to sit on them counter stools again. Belle went too far, cause she cussed Endora out bout that new girl. Endora had Mr. Niles fire Belle. I guess that was the wrong thing to do, cause the new girl didn't want no part of Endora. Didn't care was she the boss or not. Said, "I was lookin for a job when I found this one. I can look again, it don't bother me none!"

The worse part was when Belle started tellin all over town bout what Endora like to do! Endora rather anything than to let her mama hear that kinda mess. She was too lazy to whip Belle's ass, so she gave her some money and sent her off on some trip to some place Belle wanted to go for awhile. But I bet that problem ain't over! You watch! Anyway, that trouble made Endora get closer to her husband and even God, cause she was shamed. Mr. Niles happier now . . . for awhile. Specially cause that's when she got pregnant.

Surprise to say, Endora was lazy, but she seem to look forward to havin a baby. That's all she talked about. She bought just loads of things for that child, so many it probly never did get to wear em all fore it grew out of em. Yes, don't you know? Endora had another little girl! I guess girls just run in that family! She named her baby Freedora. Dora was proud again. Everybody in her family was named after her!

Strange, but good to say, Endora's mind made a change when her body did. While she was pregnant, and after the baby was born, Endora had plenty time to look around her life . . . and she saw her husband. She saw how some of them other ladies, good-lookin ones too!, looked and talked to Mr. Niles. They was after him! Now, there ain't nothin, sometimes, like seein your man through another woman's eyes! He started lookin better to her. You see? She took to not bein so lazy round him, and takin time to dress and primp up for him. Cause some of them other women looked really good. Lovin with him got better, too.

Now, I ain't in her mind, so I don't know the facts, but her actions seem to be that she grew to love him. Stopped missin a woman to love. Well, ain't nothin in the world impossible! With that baby, and bein a mother, Endora became a woman totally. At least, she ain't reached back in all this time. Maybe she was too lazy to love two people. I do know for sure that man is happier, that woman is happier and that baby is happy. Who knows bout people and they hearts? Do you?

Endora turned out to be a good mother. She quieted down some from her little sneaky ways. She was jealous of that baby. Wanted all its love for herself. Mr. Niles was beside himself, he was so happy to be a daddy! Finally, he thought, here would be a female to take his money without takin advantage of him. Would love him. He was the daddy. How that baby was able to come here and be cute, I don't know, cause she looked just like him. But she sure was cute and, now, is a good-lookin young lady.

So, that's how Endora's life was runnin bout the time they was all comin home.

Me? Well, now I had done found out that mongst my children I did have another one who liked to dream. He drew things, pictures and such. The stuff looked good to me, but I'm his mama. Yet, after bein this close to Dora and all her family, I membered bout them dreams and I took to takin all extra money I could keep my hands on and spendin it on pencils, paints and them canvas things for him.

I blived nobody would ever get to lovin him like I did. Cause he was lame. Clubfoot, one leg shorter. So, I said, let him dream, please. Dream, son. Dream and work on your dream. Please, Jesus. He loved God, too.

I'm glad I did! It ended up with him goin to the Europea place. To study. Was sent for, chile. Somebody else like his work sides me.

Another thing, I started bein real lonely. I see my old husband sometime, and, can't lie, the man made me feel so good in a bed, I just still feel somethin for him. I just don't want ALL of him! So, I guess I can't have none. I did let him sneak me off, now and again. Like he the one wanted it. But I always come home . . . alone . . . like I want. I only went twice.

I even started thinkin I might marry again. Started lookin round to see what I could see. Once when I went over to see bout how her back was doin, I told Dora bout it, you know that. I thought she would laugh and talk bout me bein weak. But, surprise to me, she didn't.

She just said, "You . . ." stopped peelin apples and started lookin out the window to the sky. It happen to be thunderin and lightnin that day, too. I members, cause the rain always make me feel like lovin. Then she said, "Life sure give a body plenty to think about in this world."

I said, "Life give your brain plenty to think bout in this world. It's Love what give your body plenty to think bout."

We, both, wasn't real old. Just tired. But we could look kinda good if we really, really would try. Well, almost good, anyway. Enough for soooommmme man! But we tired, I guess.

Then I helped her finish peelin them apples and we made us a pie, ate most of it, laughin bout life and love. Then I went home, full, and cried even tho I wasn't real sad. Just lonely.

SPLENDORA

Splendora was one of them children born bein old and young at the same time. As a real small child she was serious, takin time to think bout things, and still lovin to laugh, play and be happy.

Like Lovedora she loved all things livin, specially them what hurt in some way. Just took em to her heart. Even growin things, trees, flowers, clouds, gardens, everything. Dora had a time keepin little baby chicks, kittens and puppies outa Splendora's bed. Sneaked in. Endora always told off on her anyway.

Mongst her sisters, Lovedora loved her most the time. Windora loved her sometime. Endora loved her ever once in a while when she wasn't jealous of her. They didn't like Splendora comin late to they mama, without they papa. Said she wasn't really part of them.

200

Dora loved her special and her name was always there to prove it. Splendora was her thunder and lightnin love child.

There always seem to be some deep, kinda quiet excitement bout life in Splendora. She adventured in life! Into everything was round her and even far away as she dared go alone. She liked to be alone. Just walkin or sittin, thinkin. Tho sometime she did make my lame son, Walton, go with her. He didn't like to be out round peoples when he didn't have to be. She was sure a different kind of child. We use to wonder what was that child be thinkin so serious bout.

Now, Lovedora loved all animals, sick or well. But Splendora loved mostly the sick ones, the hurt ones. Her heart went out to em and she try to find someway to heal em or repair em, or find a home for one she couldn't keep on accounta her mama. Or her big-mouth sisters!

I done told you how she growed up to be a beautiful young woman, but she did go through a time when she didn't look like she was gonna be pretty. Her eyes was always beautiful tho. Deep, brown and shiny wet. Kind eyes, thoughtful. I blive she loved all her sisters, her family. She sure did love Dora.

Splendora cried, often times, bout things and people for no reason anybody else could see. Her nerves, or her brain, seem to "feel" things bout everything round her. Sensitive, I blive they call it, cordin to the new words I learn from my lame son who paints. She "sensed" things. Thought most everybody was sad. We laughed at her then, but as I grow older I begin to think she is right. She said even things like curtains, trees, some animals, looked sad to her. I looked this word up with my son, *vulnerable.* That's what she thought. People, too, even when they be laughin, she said.

She was smart in school. Liked to play with girls and boys. Wasn't no tomboy tho. Just like to play with em. That child even liked learnin and her teachers. Specially that blind one her mama had worked for. Splendora even stayed round that teacher when her mama didn't work there no more. When the teacher was sick, near to dyin, Splendora was always there, doin things for her. Rubbin her back, soothin her, somehow. Cookin special things for her. Readin to her. Talkin to her, they say, bout things goin on all over the world. Sometimes speakin in that foreigner speech the teacher had taught her some of.

That teacher was beautiful to Splendora. She was kinda strange lookin to me. Was a tiny little woman with a wrinkled face like a dried prune. Had a head full of dark hair she wore pulled straight back into a big, ole bun. That bun was always loose with long hairs hangin round, cause she shook her head when she got excited bout what she was teachin, which was always, when she be teachin Splendora. She shake her head and wave her arms, and sometimes in the middle of what she be sayin, she give a little laugh, a happy laugh, like her mind was bubblin over into her heart and a little had to spill out. She was blind, but she could see what she was sayin, in her heart. She was always givin Splendora things, nice things. They was friends til that teacher died. Years. Always close. She was sad when Splendora wanted to marry stead of travel. But, wellll.

Anyway, when she died, she left Splendora some little money with a note sayin, "Feed your heart, massage your mind. Travel. I'll be with you, little friend." She didn't leave her no millions, cause she didn't have much herself. But, some. Probly all her savings for bout thirty-five years of teachin work.

Splendora always spent a lot of time with my lame son who paints. He didn't paint then, just drawed on everything. They was bout the same age and she never teased him for bein lame, just liked him and treated him normal-like. Made him take them walks with her sometimes. They was always in a huddle, talkin. I loved her special for that, cause I loved him.

Now . . . as each sister left home, Splendora took over lovin her mama more, to take they place. She helped her mama in a lotta ways when they got to be alone. She was a big girl-woman then. She had her own room, but she still slept with Dora. They be in that bed laughin and talkin through the nights sometime.

One thing more, Splendora thought of God a lot. She the one went to church mostly. Didn't have to make her go. She say she blive in Him even fore she knew nothin bout Him.

That's how she met the preacher-man's son. When she finally married, that's who she married. To be closer to God, she thought. They had one problem. She like to make love outside in the sun, or under a tree in the rain, under the moon. Her husband didn't. He say too many eyes outside might see em. He want to be in a dark room. They only stayed married bout six months, cause she got to know the church better.

Splendora told her mama that she first use to think the preacher was misleadin his congregation, just makin em shout, not think! bout what God really means and wants. And beggin for money. Just ridin his cadillac round and smilin at the single sisters and some married ones too. She say she thought that til, one day, two, three months into her marriage when she was closer in the church, she overheard some of the church-sisters talkin.

The sisters was dressed-to-kill! Big, wide hats with feathers and flowers on em, hot-red and midnight-blue dresses with ribbons and bows sittin on they behinds and shoulders, feet stuffed into little sandles with toes hangin over the edges of the sole. Hair shinin, red-hot lips like slashes cross they face, earrings hangin to yonder and back. Sharp!!

They was sayin, "We got to get Reverand a new Cadillac! The Greater Pilgrim Church done got they preacher a brand new silver Cadillac! We got to get ours a gold one! Can't let em outdo us!"

Another one answered, "He need some new suits, too! When he be ridin out on his errands of mercy, he need to look good! Them last suits he got must be bout six months old now!"

Then one said, "I like my preacher to look good! He got to ride good too! Show everybody how God blesses a good man!"

The first one smiled, flashin long teeth, "Well, we just gonna have to take up a extra collection! We have to talk to these people holdin back on some of that money! We got to have a preacher we can be proud of when people see him! We ain't gonna let no other church outdo us!"

Like that. Worldly.

Then, she notice durin church meetin, the ladies in the front row sit with they knees apart, dress hiked up, just a'starin at the preacher and the deacons, who was preachin and starin back!

Splendora didn't like that. She said, "Wasn't no 'God' in

that! That ain't church. They don't leave the worldly ways outside, they bring em in!" Got so she didn't like to go to her husband's church.

Round then she got that heritance from the blind teacher-friend. She made up her mind to leave her husband. They had never let her have no money, cept for food shoppin, so when she left she thought she deserved some money to take with her.

Now, whenever Splendora handed the church collection plate around, the people put more money in it, thinkin she would tell the preacher who was givin what, so she always took in a good collection. This particular Sunday she took collection from front of church to back. When she through with that back row, she took the other collection plate from the one collectin on the other side of the church rows and poured it into her plate. Now durin the meetin collection time, the preacher, piano player and choir get to singin and shoutin real hard to get the givers excited, make em dig deeper in they pockets. By time Splendora got through the last row, the people was kinda shouting and happy! Splendora took the whole plate and all, went on out the doors of the church and came on home to Dora. I think she had bout $270.

The preacher, his wife and son come bustin by right after church let out. Didn't even stay to shake hands with the congregation. They want they money! Splendora say she didn't have "they" money, she only had hers. She wouldn't come out and Dora wouldn't let em in. Dora kept tellin them to go or she gonna call the police. They kept sayin Splendora a thief! And they gonna call the police right back! Neither one did. They finally went away. Preacher cussin and mad at his son for marryin up with "one of them dumb doras!" Son didn't know whether to stay and beg or to go. Cause he had family in both directions. But Splendora told him to go cause she was already gone! He finally left. Didn't want nobody hearin him beggin no woman to come home.

The preacher-man's son sat, waitin for her to come beggin back, said god was on his side. Well, Splendora wasn't.

Splendora told God, "I didn't take no money from you. It wasn't gonna be spent on you noway. I took it from my husband. He owe it to me. So . . . I'm not stealin."

After that she was gone, gone. Got her heritance, gave her mama some. Visited her sister in Chicago for to get some clothes, then went far as we could even think of . . . to Europea. Windora said she bought plenty clothes. Dora said that money must sure be gone.

With Windora's help, Splendora knew some places to go in Europea. She took a room and bath in a very nice hotel in Paris. Her money sounded big to her, well, she hadn't never had any. But, in bout a month or two, them French had done eaten it almost all up.

She wrote her mama regular most times. And the money mighta been gone, but she sure found some to send home to her mama from time to time. Dora grieved for her, missed her last baby gone from home . . . alone.

Dora beg Lovedora to send Pandora to stay with her awhile. She come, but she soon gone, cause her mama got that TB and she needed at home. Then she beg Windora for Goldora, but she didn't let her come cept in the summers sometime. Endora told her mama she could come over there anytime and see Freedora, but Dora want to hold somebody at night while she sleep. Anyway . . . the years passed.

Over the years, she got letters from Splendora from all kinds of places. My son Walton, the lame one who had dreams, got letters sometimes too. Once or twice we didn't hear nothin for a long time. Then she wrote and ask bout my son Walton again. Was he still wantin to paint? Said she had a way for him to come there and study art! That's when my boy, man now, was leavin me. We cried. But I was glad he was dreamin and bout to get that dream! Just he didn't come back, he stayed. Learned and learned. Til Splendora came back, bout ten more years later. He got to where he even sent me some money! But I wanted him back! They was both bout thirty-four and thirty-five when they come home, cause me and Dora was bout goin on fifty-nine, sixty. But I done got way head of my story.

At first, Splendora just enjoy bein a lady. She say them mens love black women over there! She change her clothes, couldn't wait to wear em, I guess, two, three times a day! I blive they couldn't quite make out what she was all about!

Mens try to meet her when she go out for walks in that huge monstrous city, or when she at her dinner table back at her hotel. At first she didn't be too friendly with em, didn't want em to get the wrong idea. But you got to be friends with somebody, so she made friends with the elevator man, always goin up or down, you see.

They talked on the short rides. Then . . . he start makin them smiles and words which mean, "I want to jugie-jugie with you." Splendora just laughed at his nerve and say, "I'm a Christian woman." He offer the Christian woman money, say, "I give you fifty francs." Went from there to a hundred francs to a hundred fifty francs! Then he got mad at her cause it was too much and she still say, no. He still smile tho.

Men see him talkin to her and ask him bout her. He say, "She not a prostitute. She his friend. She don't want to talk to anyone else." This make them men try harder to make her one. Either just for themself or everybody. Ain't it funny how all over the world, life is kinda the same?

Well, you know, that money was finally gone. Most of it. Splendora had done been tryin to get a work permit or somethin, but seems it was really hard to get. She kept tryin cause she really need work and money now. She also hadn't been able to find a cheap apartment either. She wrote us that cheap hotels were too dangerous for her, alone.

One day, very soon, she count her money layin in that bag with the ticket home. She didn't want to come home broke and with nothin from Paris. And that week her rent would be behind too!

So she took to ridin that elevator to get that elevator man to ask her again, to offer her them francs. (That's what they call their money.) That ole geezer musta been able to read her mind and pockets. Cause where he always ask her, again, everytime she get on his elevator and be alone, this time he didn't say nothin, just smiled at her. Knew she was in a tight spot and that was his chance! Finally, after bout the tenth ride that day and he ain't said nothin, she did say somethin.

She smiled, said, "The money you offered me . . . I think . . . I blive I will take it. I need it very much."

What she say that for!? "I NEED it very much." That ole thing of his must have leaped in his drawers. He smiled, said, "Oh! The money. Well . . ." He laughed a ugly, little, gray laugh, "Well now. I don't have so much money now. I have only a hundred francs. See? I told you you should say yes! When I had it!"

She said, "A hundred francs be alright cause I have to pay my rent. Then maybe my job will come through." They was at her floor then, so she had to get out. She tried to ask, "How will we . . ."

He laughed and shut the door, sayin, "I let you know." He was gone.

She sat by her phone. He didn't call. She got back on the elevator. He laughed again. She said, "How . . ."

He said, "I count my money. I only have fifty francs to spend. I am poor man."

She look down at her feet, say, "Well . . . okey. I need it." Time for her to get out again. She ask, again, "How will . . ."

He laugh that ugly, gray laugh again, reach to touch her behind, she hit his hand, he reached for her breast, she let him a second or two, then she move his hand away. He laughed, "I let you know." Then he shut the door and was gone.

That happen til the money was down to twenty francs. Splendora didn't want to take it. But she had to. Didn't know nowhere to go where they help beautifully dressed women from America! Didn't really know nobody but him, the elevator man.

He finally ran into her room. She lay back and spread her legs. He did what he came for. Left eighteen francs on her table and was gone. Lucky she got that!

Splendora got up, cleaned up. Felt dirty. Said, "Lord. What is going to be next for me? I don't want to do this, but what am I gonna do? Help me. Help me out of this. Please. Do I have to go home? To nothin, with nothin? I'm willin to work. Help me get a job so I never have to do this again. Please Lord, please. I have stolen. Now, I have whored. Oh! God! I am sorry! Help me!"

That sellin business tore her up a little. She was hurt, not in her body, it only felt dirty from that ugly little elevator man. She was hurt in her heart and mind. She had hated it when Lovedora went through it. Thought Lovedora was a fool. Well, Lovedora was! She gave her money away. Splendora was keepin hers, usin it herself! If you gonna do a dirty job like that, you need to keep any money from it for yourself. Don't give your soul away!

She stayed in her room that night and the next few days, eatin sandwitches she ran out and bought, goin down the stairs. She thought everybody would be starin at her, talkin bout her. Finally she said to hell with it and went down to dinner dressed in her best best dress. She looked beautiful. She said if they put her out, she would look good goin. She was almost to the dessert when the waiter brought her a card from a gentleman askin could he join her.

Now, just to let you know what happened. After the elevator man had brought her down (he thought), he talked bout how he had done so good to the barman. A gentleman was at the bar he didn't think too much of cause he was a midget, a dwarf, so he didn't pay him no tention and the gentleman heard his story. He didn't know the dwarf gentleman owned the hotel cause the dwarf didn't let everybody know his business. This hotel was just one of the places his family had left him. He had a'plenty! After the dwarf heard the whole story bout how long Splendora had held out, he sat in his usual office in another buildin he owned and thought about this beautiful woman holdin out and finally givin in to a elevator man cause she was in need. He thought about his own life. Few thrills in it. Him bein shy and self-conscious bout his size. But that trick she turned brought her down to his size in a way. Sides that, she was beautiful, black, alone and in need. Different. Seeked after. Waited til the end fore she took that road down. He looked at it that way.

That evening the dwarf went back to that hotel, sat drinkin coffee and liquor til she came down. He was bout to give up and go when she finally came down for dinner. She had done planned not to come down, but finally her stomach got the best of her and she could sign for her meals there. She sat down thinkin everybody lookin at her again. That's when the dwarf man sent his card with his name only on it, askin to join her.

Now . . . Splendora was sad and feelin just so alone, so, she thought, what the hell? Why not? and told the waiter Yes, he could join her. He did. She was so shocked to see this little man, dressed so neat and rich-like. Cane and all. She just couldn't hardly talk. He didn't talk much either. He shame too, I guess, for askin. But great big bells was ringin in his stomach. And little bitty bells was ringin in her brain. They stumbled over a few beginnin words.

Then, after awhile, he ask to pay for her check. She nodded gratefully. He did.

He told her he would like to dine with her every night while he in town and when he couldn't make it, to have dinner as his guest anyway. (He didn't want to give nobody else the chance that elevator man had had.) She couldn't not blive her ears! He hadn't ask her for nothin! He didn't, either.

That went on for bout a week. Splendora runnin back and forth tween the work-permit office, her room and fear. He was the only good thing in her life at that time. And by that time, they was laughin and talkin better. He told her he had paid her hotel bill. That she might like to move to a small apartment he had found, it would be cheaper. She hadn't been able to find one. I'm tellin you it sound like a fairy tale, but these things must do happen sometime in real life.

Splendora swallowed her food, took a deep breath, sighed and said, "Why? Why are you doin all this for me?" Wasn't she foolish?

He answered, throwing his hands into the air, "Why not? I have the money. You have not. I like you. You are a clean woman. Your mind is not ruined. You are . . . different. You are American. Most important, you are a beautiful woman. You were born to be taken care of. I would like a . . . companion. Don't worry, I will not ask too much of you. Just this one thing. . . . Never . . . NEVER . . . have another man in your life as long as I keep you."

Well, you know, that suited Splendora fine. But she thought of havin this little man who she did not love either. She did not want too many sins on her back.

Well, it turned out that this dwarf man could not have a woman either. But he wanted to love one, own one nobody else could have, to extablish his manhood amongst other men. Splendora thought this was a blessin. I ain't sure, but I guess it was.

He sent her out shoppin, made her charge accounts. Put

her in that apartment. She passed that elevator man without even turnin her eyes his way. That man wanted to smirk, cause he thought he had brought her down, but she didn't give him a chance. And, now, no one would ever blive him noway.

A few days later, Splendora and the dwarf left for Monte Carlo. She was one of the most beautiful women there. And baby clean. No one knew her. He liked that. None could have her. He loved that. She was his, alone. And that man dressed her, gave her jewels, furs, everything she wanted. From then on to the next fourteen years, that's how she lived. I told you Splendora was splendid.

Splendora traveled on yachts, flew in private planes, all over the world cept the United States. She went to Africa. Of course she got real lonely bout four or five years down the line. And one time in Monte Carlo again, a king sent her a note and a diamond what wasn't set in nothin! That was the time she decided to go all the way no matter bout the dwarf. She let that king have her in his own suite. It was done with great beauty and much money spent, but she never went back nor did that kind of thing again. Just cause he was a king I guess, even tho he didn't have no place to be king of no more. Well, she was only a woman what had dreamed.

Then, lonely again, she thought of Walton who wanted to paint. My son. She wrote us and she sent for him and sent him to school. The little man did not like that, but he allowed it cause Walton was never with them.

Now this little man had a family too! Somebody his family had wanted him married to. But he kept Splendora.

Wisest thing Splendora did was save her money. Sent it home to her mama to save for her. She had them diamonds and furs and goo-gobs of clothes, beautiful clothes. She lived in what looked like a beautiful palace. She wished her old blind teacher could see her. You know what I mean. She could speak bout two or three of them different languages even. Yes, Splendora was splendid.

But . . . she never made love in all those years. Don't count the king, she didn't love him. The little man only like to lay beside her, naked, and just stroke her body. He musta loved her by then. Once he yelled, "It's hard! It's hard!" But it didn't stay that way long. So, they went back to strokin again . . . for years.

Finally Splendora got real lonely for her mama. Walton was not through studyin, that can go on and on, he say. But he was sellin things. Gettin kinda famous! My son! So . . . Splendora decided it was time to come home.

Now, Walton came home when Splendora did, but she also brought that little man with her. Can't tell you who he was cause I can't say, nor spell, his name. I called him "Man." He let me. Seem to like that name. Could tell he had money, just somethin bout his clothes and his ways. He turned his nose up at everything less it was the Best! Don't know if he liked our cookin tho. Splendora could cook whatever he wanted, and she did. I blive he musta loved Splendora cause he watched her all the time. He use to look at Walton kinda hard too.

Anyway . . . Splendora was home, at last! She and her mama lay in bed again and talked bout all what Splendora had done since she left. Not everything, I guess, just what Splendora might want to let her mama know. Dora say it was like bein on the trip herself. She say her daughter had done all such things, and more, that she would always want to do.

But she thought, too, that Splendora had done some things wrong. Mama's got sense!

Splendora say, "I been all over every place almost in the world that money will take you. Sometimes it's like paradise, sometimes it's like hell. I've seen so much! I'm tired, weary even, from what all I've seen. I feel like I have lived a thousand lives. I . . . been so many things . . . done . . . so many things." She look up at Dora with them bright, beautiful eyes. "I been rich, Mama! You know, cause I sent you that money." Her eyes go sad on us. "I've been poor, too. Long time ago. You remember when I didn't send you none?" Then she light up again. "I dressed in the very best of clothes designed by the very best designers in Paris and Rome, as well as Windora's!" She laughed. "Couldn't forget my sister over here!"

Another time, she say, "I can speak four languages, Mama!"

Dora say, "Do em for me." And Splendora would. We loved it even if we couldn't make nothin out of what she sayin! We laughed a lot with Splendora, just bein happy to be round her!

But, sometimes, Splendora cried as her mama held her in her arms. Sayin, "Mama, I was sad so much, and I had to go through things I don't like to talk about. Then, again, one day I would look up and be sitting drinking champagne on some yacht. Sailing in the most beautiful waters in the world, around the islands of Greece. Eating foods brought from some of the fartherest places in the world. The most expensive food in the world. The ice in my drink would be from an iceberg! Me!"

One day she turned from the window she liked to look

out of, smiled sadly, said, "Mama, I was one of the most beautiful women in Monte Carlo. Once. All the men sent champagne and orchids, jewels and furs, trying to meet me. I had to send them back . . . all but one. Her voice got low and breathless, "Mama, I've been made love to by a king! One with no country left to be king of, it's true. But king never-the-less!" She turn back to the window a while. Then she say, "But I've been to the bottom, too. Been made love to by a elevator man once. So I could eat." She turn away again, sayin, "Neither time didn't make me nothin splendid!" This time she don't turn back to us. Just sit, stare out that window and think.

Another time when she happier, she say, "I've been to Africa, Mama. Africa! Exploring. I've been to the top of the Alps. I've flown over snow-capped mountains and over jungles no man nor woman has walked in. Mama, I've seen so much beauty on this earth." Then she get sad again. "And really been to hell, so much pain in the people on this earth."

Another time she told Dora, "Mama, I'm tryin to make up my mind about some things I want to do, need to do, don't know if I can do them or not."

Dora said, "Tell me, see can I help you think bout it."

Splendora kissed her mama, said, "It's my life. Nobody can decide this particular thing but me." Then she changed the subject, I guess.

One time when she was even more serious, she said, "One day I woke up, on my satin sheets. The lace and silk from my designer sleeping-gown falling softly, beautiful, over my body. An empty champagne crystal glass on my white, hand-carved bedside table, neath my expensive, ancient chinese lamp. Got up, sat my feet down on my dusky Aubusson carpet, one of the finest in the world. And I realized . . . I had nothing . . . but money. Money and memories of the same things over and over. Nothing else! I didn't really KNOW me anymore! Me? Who was I really? What did I want, really want, to do? What was I going to be doing in twenty years, if I lived, when my beauty was gone? I knew of such beautiful women who had such hard times even WITH beauty. I could imagine what life would be like when it was all I depended on and it was gone. I don't want those hard times in my life! And sometimes the good times cost too much!" Dora didn't know did she want me to hear all this, but I wasn't goin nowhere! I'm a woman too! And Splendora was talkin bout a woman's kinda life I would never know!

I wouldn't look at Dora as Splendora went on talkin.

Said, "I have no children. No real home . . . except yours, and that belongs to everybody. I have no chilllld. My life is costing me, in my youth that is goin away, fading . . . fast. It is costing me too much to be free! Now . . . I want a home. My home. I'm tired. Weary of the past." She looked up into both our eyes, smiled, said, "And I am in love!"

Dora gasped, "With that strange man in there sleepin?"

Splendora shook her head, "No. I'll tell you when the time is right. I got a few things to do first before I can get to that part of me."

Dora sat back and heaved a sigh. "I hope it don't mean you goin way again for another ten, fifteen years. Do, I won't be live to see you when you come back. Doctor say my kidneys not gonna let me be here much longer. Daughter, just stay with me a little while. Let me love you close to me where I can see you."

Splendora leaned toward Dora. "Mama, you still got that land, where we all have one acre?"

Dora smiled, proud, "Ye . . . as! It's worth more now. Town finally moved that way a bit. But I didn't never sell it. Just kept payin the taxes on it. It's still you all's land. The onliest thing I can leave you all."

Splendora laughed, "No, it isn't the only thing you leaving us. You gave us plenty good sense, whether we used it or not!"

Well, they went out to see that land. The Man went with em. When they got back, Splendora was all excited. She called all kinda mens from that bigger city close round here and the next month or so, they was busy out there. Pretty soon they had plans and builders and Man was helpin pay for them to build four houses in a row on them acres. They was gonna let Endora build her own on her acre. But they thought they better build one for Windora cause she was most blind and her business was sufferin. They knew Lovedora needed a home, no question bout it! So they built em!

Splendora had the biggest and best one, with her a swimmin pool gonna be in back. Dora had the next biggest one, with rooms for her grandchildren, and they put her lawn and garden in first.

Dora secretly told me she wasn't never gonna get to live there cause she didn't spect to live. She tried to talk Splendora out of buildin one for her, just spread it out tween all the daughters, but Splendora said she knew what she was doin cause she had already talked to Dora's doctor. Dora

218

told her, "He musta lied to you! I know bout my own health! What did he say?"

All Splendora said was, "I know what I'm doin," and went on doin it!

Talk about a dream! When them houses was finished they was beautiful. They was all painted a creamy white, but they had different trims. Splendora's was lavender, Lovedora's was blue, of course, Windora's was left so she could order her own, after all, she did have some money! Dora said she wanted dark green, like her trees was gonna be. I'm tellin you they was beautiful!

Made me hate to go to my little ole, old house I still rent. Bet I done paid for it by now, for the landlord. But my son Walton, the lame one?, told me, "Don't worry, Mother." (He talk so proper now, he call me "Mother".) Said, "I have some plans. I am not working just for the pleasure. There will be some changes made here." He in that room, justa always paintin on them boards all the time! I don't care what he do, I just want him home with me!

After everything was all finished, Splendora and the Man, who had done tried to pay for most everything, they walked round the buildins. Splendora justa runnin here one minute, there another minute, lovin everything, the little Man grabbed her arm, sayin, "Now . . . this is all complete. We have to go home now."

Splendora bent down and threw her arms round his neck, said, "No. No! I want to be home, here."

The little man turned his head to the side, lookin at her, "I cannot stay here, this is not my home, not my land, these are not my ways. You must come home with me. You said you only want to come 'see' your mama." He had a funny way of sayin "mama."

Splendora dropped her arms, said, "Oh . . . my dear, dearest friend. I cannot go back to that life. You have a wife . . . and I want a man, a life of my own. I . . . I . . . want to be happy!"

Man held on to her. "Only a fool asks for happiness in this foolish, worn world. We are . . . content . . . together. That is enough for awhile."

Splendora stepped back from him, turned her head to the side, said, "Everything I have done in the last fifteen years has been for 'awhile.' I'm ready to have forever. I want to get close to my . . . God again. I want my man and my own, whatever it is. Rich or poor. I want my own."

The little man just looked at her.

She went on talkin. "I . . . love you. In . . . my own way. But . . . I've been taught by you, so . . . I want my own. My mother is getting old. I have no child. Even if I were to have a child by you . . . it would be a bastard. I don't mind bastard, I am a bastard. I just don't want a lie, when I can have the real thing! I want to stay home, here. My home . . . you have built for me. I will love you for that. Forever. But . . . I want to be loved."

He answered, "And I love you!"

Again, it was her turn to look to the side. "I mean . . . loved . . . with my body."

The little man didn't give up yet. "You are a fool! To wish to stay here in this forsaken place. Is love here? Don't be a fool! I must return to my home, my business. If you wish to return . . . soon . . . you may call on me. But it must be SOON! Don't wait . . . too long."

The next day Man flew out from the nearest airport. Their last words were:

Him, "I think you have used me."

Her, "We have used each other."

Him, "I think you may be overpaid."

Her, "You do not like used or cheap. And I was . . . not paid. I care for you. How can you pay for that? I was more than willing."

He, "With lies . . . who knows? Be happy with . . . the loved one." They looked into each other's eyes just before he turned to go. He handed her a package. She kissed him. Said, "There are a million like me for you."

He said, "You cannot count for my heart."

Then he was gone.

Durin the time of the buildin, Lovedora had moved back home with two of her children, Pandora and a son. The two other boys was workin on little jobs they had, while the time ran out for the bank to take the house. They was gonna drive up in their dad's old car later.

Lovedora was coughin a lot, that little dry cough with the specks of blood endin up on them clean white rags that Dora kept up for her. Dora cried over that child practly dyin in fronta her eyes. Lovedora had lost a lot of weight! Didn't have much to start with. Splendora looked at her and shook her head sadly. Said, "Hold on, sister, hold on."

Then Windora came. Goldora brought her, then went on back to school somewhere. I know it was a good school cause it was private. Windora couldn't sew anymore, cept sometimes in the mornin light, her eyesight was so bad. Was really blind, cept for one eye that as she used it, got dimmer and dimmer through the day. She had money, but she was goin blind right on. Nothin the doctors could do, she said, and she couldn't get no new eyes.

Endora was already here, you know that, and she was always over to see her sisters. To admire their clothes, all cept Lovedora, who only had love, mmh! mmh! Sometimes a person don't know what to do, one way or another. Anyway, Endora was gettin all her information bout schools and things for Freedora. She wanted the best for her, she said.

Dora was mostly layin down with her back trouble what come from her kidneys what the doctor said was tryin to fail. She love to watch her children. Them that had dreamed and done something in their own way. Her eyes just fill up with tears, but she was happy. She sure would love to live in that beautiful house with her daughters, Lovedora and Splendora, and whatever grandchild she could get hold to. In her heart, she didn't blive she was gonna live long enough to do none of that!

Now! So much was happenin all at one time, if I say it all together you never would understand what I was talkin bout! So, I have to tell you all one thing at a time. Just keep in mind it all happen at bout the same time!

Chile! All them Doras!

First, I was so glad to have my artist son home. He was happy! Clubfoot, short leg and all! Thank God! He did beautiful work and showed me catalogues of his work in different places in Europea. Said soon America might know him. He had brought me two beautiful big picture-paintings. They was too beautiful for my house. One was a sunrise over water someplace in Italy, he said, Port-oh-something, and the other was of trees and a wide street with busy, good-lookin people, in Paris, he say. And he had put me in that one! There I was walkin down that street I hadn't done ever seen! He said I could go there if I want to! Someday. Chile, I ain't never gonna fly over all that water! Sides, I'm already there in that picture-paintin! If I wanna lie I can prove I been to Paris cause you can see me right there!

Then . . . my dentist and veterary came. Lord, them three children was happy to see each other. I looked at them and cried, thinkin of the ones I had lost. The other three of mine, livin, that had never had no dreams came over, but they didn't get along with each other too good. They want to fuss and talk smart bout my dreamer children tryin to be uppity or somethin! Chile, I don't know bout blood bein thicker all the time.

Round that time Splendora took to goin to some special doctors over at the city just outa town here. Then bout three weeks later, she had Dora, Lovedora and Windora go with her.

Now . . . here's what happen. Splendora was plannin the whole thing. She was payin for everything! Probly with what that Man had give her in that package he left. In another month . . . they was all goin in the hospital. Splendora first. Then Lovedora. Seems Splendora was gonna give up a lung from her beautiful body for her sister so she could live. She did that.

Then bout a month later Windora went to the hospital. Splendora was gonna give up a eye from that beautiful face for her sister so she could see. She did that.

Last, Dora went. Splendora had them take one of her kidneys from her now cut-up beautiful body, so her mama could live a little longer, if it took. It took. Splendora did that.

Earlier, they had tried to fight her doin that, but they was happy in their hearts. Who don't want to live?

Love, love, love. What won't it do!? Oh Lord, Jesus and God!

Well, that all took bout three months more. When it was all over, they rolled each one, Lovedora first, into that new house to get well. Her kids was there to help her. Good thing, they was home! Soon some color and life was back in Lovedora's sad, happy face. She was gonna do fine!

By time Windora came home, Goldora just demanded to be there with her mama from school. Windora was so happy bout that eye, she cried, til the doctor told her to stop or she could ruin that good eye she just got. She stopped. Dried right up. Mostly.

Dora came home on a stretcher. Her and Splendora stayed the longest in the hospital. But finally they let Dora out. Endora was payin somebody to take care of her right. Even makin Freedora help cause it's her family too!

Splendora finally came home, bout a month later after Dora. They had held her the longest cause her body had been in shock or somethin! Everybody was all in the hall waitin for her. Dora was in a wheelchair. They brought Splendora home in a wheel chair. My son, Walton, was there. I wish I could tell you so you could see what I'm tryin to say. Everybody in some little pain, gettin well, happy and sad at the same time. Cryin for joy. Chile, chile.

Splendora was rolled into her lovely hallway and they was all there, waitin. You could hear sniffin, wheezin and shufflin goin on. Splendora was worn, thin, weary and tired, but . . . she was smilin. Dried blood specks on her arms and sleeves where they done used them needles givin her things to build her up, keep her well, feed her. She in a little white robe with bandages all round her chest and back. You could see some bruises different places where that robe fell off a little. Even her slippers had little dried bits of blood and things on em. Her one eye was open bright, smilin like her lips. The other eye was wrinkled, closed and sunk in a bit. But the face! That face was happy . . . and still smilin . . . tho you sure could tell she had suffered and was in a little pain.

I was so proud of her. So happy for them, for my friend. I blive I loved Splendora better than my own children for a minute. Oh! Splendora was splendid! She was!

There Lovedora was, a little bent over, with her back still bandaged a bit, wheezin a little, her body gettin used to that new lung that was workin! There Windora was, bandages all round her head. Less now than last month. No eyes showin yet, arms stretched out to her sister who had give her new sight. She was cryin again, askin somebody to hand her to Splendora.

Dora tryin to get out her wheel chair to take her Splendora in her arms. My son, Walton, held her down and wheeled them two chairs together, they grabbed each other's hand and held on, tight. Patted each other with the other hand. Everybody else huggin them and each other too. Oh, it was a sight full of so much love. Not just cause they was a family, cause every family don't do them things. This was love just cause somebody was made that way.

Endora was cryin, screamin, "I wanna give somebody

somethin! I wanna give somebody somethin! Nobody didn't ask me!"

I told her, "Didn't nobody ask Splendora. Your time might come, girl. You got a big family!" I was surprised when she hugged me. Love is catchin sometimes.

Then, surprised me, my son Walton bent over, took Splendora's hands and bent some more to kiss those dry, cracked lips. Then I knew he loved her. She smiled up at him. He knelt down, said to her, "It's all done now. You are through with that dream." She kept smilin and put her hand on his face, her head on his shoulder. See ain't nothin cripple bout him but his foot!

He turned to us, said, "Look here, you all. I want you to meet my future wife. We are gettin married soon as she can stand up." She raised her head and smiled and the sun came out in that hall. Then I knew she loved him. My dear, clubfoot, cripple son who I never thought would ever be loved. Oh, where did Splendora get her heart?

True to the words, when all was over and everybody was up and gettin round good, Walton and Splendora came down the aisle. Him, limpin and handsome in his tuxedo. Her with one eye (new one not in yet), back caved in on one side, in a beautiful lavender off-the-shoulder dress Windora had designed and had made for her. Her back scar showed a little bit. But . . . that little bent, cut, limpin couple look like they was the most beautiful, happiest people in the world. Everybody had a good time at the reception!

They moved into the new house. Well, Walton did. Cause Splendora was already there fixin up a studio for him to do his work in.

You may not blive this, after all Splendora had put her body through. But in a year, Splendora had a baby. Yes, you guess right. It was a girl. They named her Alldora. I said to myself, "Another Dora. Mmh! Mmh!"

Me? Well . . . I got so much family now, I'm givin up marryin again. Not cause I'm too old. I'm just already happy. I love my family and my dearest friend, Dora. We all in the same family now! I'm part of a family goin SOME-WHERE! I'm proud to be close to her . . . out of all the people in this great big huge world.

Let me tell you somethin else makes me happy, made Dora happy too. This year, when my doctor-dentist daughter had her a baby, she let me name it. I bet you laughin, thinkin bout what I would name it. I sure wouldn't name it after me, my name is Rosie Mae. Ain't that nothin!?

Well, I'll tell you what I named it. Things bein like they is, there is only one thing I COULD name that baby. I said to myself, there ain't never been nothin in my life like a Dora. Maybe it will give my grandbaby somethin good, like they give to me. She a strong, lusty little girl. I watch her eyes, can see her thinkin already, can see she ain't gonna be no fool.

So, yes, that's what I named her. A dora.

Adora!

So, maybe here we go again.

ABOUT THE AUTHOR

J. California Cooper is the author of three collections of stories—*Some Soul to Keep, Homemade Love* (a recipient of the 1989 American Book Award), and *A Piece of Mine*—as well as a novel, *Family*, and seventeen plays, many of which have been produced and performed on the stage, public television, radio, and college campuses. Her plays have also been anthologized, and in 1978 she was named Black Playwright of the Year for *Strangers*, which was performed at the San Francisco Palace of Fine Arts. Among her numerous awards are the James Baldwin Writing Award (1988) and the Literary Lion Award from the American Library Association (1988). Ms. Cooper lives in a small town in Texas, and is the mother of a daughter, Paris Williams.